the most fun a kid could have on a rainy afternoon or the best thing an adult could enjoy after a long day at work.

Pick up a volume, and remember what reading is supposed to be all about. Remember curling up with a *great story*.

—Kevin J. Anderson

KEVIN J. ANDERSON *is the author of more than ninety critically acclaimed works of speculative fiction, including* The Saga of Seven Suns, *the continuation of the* Dune Chronicles *with Brian Herbert, and his* New York Times *bestselling novelization of L. Ron Hubbard's* Ai! Pedrito!

D0916132

A Matter of Matter

L. RON HUBBARD

A Matter of Matter

GALAXY PRESS

Published by
Galaxy Press, LLC
7051 Hollywood Boulevard, Suite 200
Hollywood, CA 90028

Printed in the United States of America.

ISBN-10 1-59212-366-X
ISBN-13 978-1-59212-366-7

Library of Congress Control Number: 2007903179

Contents

Stories from Pulp Fiction's Golden Age

AND it *was* a golden age.

The 1930s and 1940s were a vibrant, seminal time for a gigantic audience of eager readers, probably the largest per capita audience of readers in American history. The magazine racks were chock-full of publications with ragged trims, garish cover art, cheap brown pulp paper, low cover prices—and the most excitement you could hold in your hands.

"Pulp" magazines, named for their rough-cut, pulpwood paper, were a vehicle for more amazing tales than Scheherazade could have told in a million and one nights. Set apart from higher-class "slick" magazines, printed on fancy glossy paper with quality artwork and superior production values, the pulps were for the "rest of us," adventure story after adventure story for people who liked to *read*. Pulp fiction authors were no-holds-barred entertainers—real storytellers. They were more interested in a thrilling plot twist, a horrific villain or a white-knuckle adventure than they were in lavish prose or convoluted metaphors.

The sheer volume of tales released during this wondrous golden age remains unmatched in any other period of literary history—hundreds of thousands of published stories in over nine hundred different magazines. Some titles lasted only an issue or two; many magazines succumbed to paper shortages during World War II, while others endured for decades yet. Pulp fiction remains as a treasure trove of stories you can read, stories you can love, stories you can remember. The stories were driven by plot and character, with grand heroes, terrible villains, beautiful damsels (often in distress), diabolical plots, amazing places, breathless romances. The readers wanted to be taken beyond the mundane, to live adventures far removed from their ordinary lives—and the pulps rarely failed to deliver.

In that regard, pulp fiction stands in the tradition of all memorable literature. For as history has shown, good stories are much more than fancy prose. William Shakespeare, Charles Dickens, Jules Verne, Alexandre Dumas—many of the greatest literary figures wrote their fiction for the readers, not simply literary colleagues and academic admirers. And writers for pulp magazines were no exception. These publications reached an audience that dwarfed the circulations of today's short story magazines. Issues of the pulps were scooped up and read by over thirty million avid readers each month.

Because pulp fiction writers were often paid no more than a cent a word, they had to become prolific or starve. They also had to write aggressively. As Richard Kyle, publisher and editor of *Argosy,* the first and most long-lived of the pulps, so pointedly explained: "The pulp magazine writers, the best of them, worked for markets that did not write for critics or attempt to satisfy timid advertisers. Not having to answer to anyone other than their readers, they wrote about human beings on the edges of the unknown, in those new lands the future would explore. They wrote for what we would become, not for what we had already been."

Some of the more lasting names that graced the pulps include H. P. Lovecraft, Edgar Rice Burroughs, Robert E. Howard, Max Brand, Louis L'Amour, Elmore Leonard, Dashiell Hammett, Raymond Chandler, Erle Stanley Gardner, John D. MacDonald, Ray Bradbury, Isaac Asimov, Robert Heinlein—and, of course, L. Ron Hubbard.

In a word, he was among the most prolific and popular writers of the era. He was also the most enduring—hence this series—and certainly among the most legendary. It all began only months after he first tried his hand at fiction, with L. Ron Hubbard tales appearing in *Thrilling Adventures, Argosy, Five-Novels Monthly, Detective Fiction Weekly, Top-Notch, Texas Ranger, War Birds, Western Stories,* even *Romantic Range.* He could write on any subject, in any genre, from jungle explorers to deep-sea divers, from G-men and gangsters, cowboys and flying aces to mountain climbers, hard-boiled detectives and spies. But he really began to shine when he turned his talent to science fiction and fantasy of which he authored nearly fifty novels or novelettes to forever change the shape of those genres.

Following in the tradition of such famed authors as Herman Melville, Mark Twain, Jack London and Ernest Hemingway, Ron Hubbard actually lived adventures that his own characters would have admired—as an ethnologist among primitive tribes, as prospector and engineer in hostile climes, as a captain of vessels on four oceans. He even wrote a series of articles for *Argosy,* called "Hell Job," in which he lived and told of the most dangerous professions a man could put his hand to.

Finally, and just for good measure, he was also an accomplished photographer, artist, filmmaker, musician and educator. But he was first and foremost a *writer,* and that's the L. Ron Hubbard we come to know through the pages of this volume.

This library of Stories from the Golden Age presents the best of L. Ron Hubbard's fiction from the heyday of storytelling, the Golden Age of the pulp magazines. In these eighty volumes, readers are treated to a full banquet of 153 stories, a kaleidoscope of tales representing every imaginable genre: science fiction, fantasy, western, mystery, thriller, horror, even romance—action of all kinds and in all places.

Because the pulps themselves were printed on such inexpensive paper with high acid content, issues were not meant to endure. As the years go by, the original issues of every pulp from *Argosy* through *Zeppelin Stories* continue crumbling into brittle, brown dust. This library preserves the L. Ron Hubbard tales from that era, presented with a distinctive look that brings back the nostalgic flavor of those times.

L. Ron Hubbard's Stories from the Golden Age has something for every taste, every reader. These tales will return you to a time when fiction was good clean entertainment and

A Matter of Matter

A Matter of Matter

Y OU have seen the gaudy little shops along Broadway.
Well, this is a warning not to patronize them.

Planets can be bought perfectly legally from the Interior
Department of the Outer Galactic Control and you don't
have to follow up the ads you read and hear over the radio;
for no matter what they say, there is many a man who would
be in much better health today if he had not succumbed to:

IT'S A POOR MAN
WHO ISN'T KING
IN SOME CORNER.
EMPIRES FOR A PITTANCE.
THRONES FOR A MITE.

Easy Payments, Nothing Down.
Honest Mike

It sounds so simple, it is so simple. Who would not be an
Earthman in this vital day? But who would be a fool?

Chuck Lambert was not exactly a fool. He was top-heavy.
He let his imagination sweep away all such things as petty
logic, shaped up the facts into something which satisfied his
dreams and went merrily along, auto-blinded to anything

3

which shadowed what he wanted to believe. Lady Luck, that mischievous character, is sometimes patient with a fool—and sometimes she loads with buckshot and lets him have it.

When he was eighteen Chuck Lambert, having precociously finished college, got a job moving packing cases and found, after six months of it, that his boss, a septuagenarian named Coley, received exactly three dollars a day more than Chuck and had had to wait forty years for his advancement. This was a blow. Chuck had visions of being president of the company at the age of twenty-four until he discovered this. The president was taking some glandular series or other and was already ninety and would live another hundred years.

Discouragement lasted just long enough to call Chuck's attention to Madman Murphy, the King of Planetary Realtors, whose magnificent display, smooth conversation, personal pounciness and assumption that Chuck had decided before he had closed a deal, opened wide the gates to glory.

Chuck was to work hard and invest every dime he could scrape into Project 19453X. This included, when it would at last be paid for, a full and clear deed of title, properly recorded and inviolate to the end of time to heirs and assigns forever, to the Planet 19453X. Murphy threw in as the clincher, free rental of a Star-Jumper IV and all supplies for the initial trip.

When he was out on the sidewalk, Chuck suddenly realized that it was going to take him eleven years of very hard work to pay for that planet, providing he starved himself the while and had no dates, and he went back in to reason with Madman Murphy.

"Look, Mr. Murphy, it stands to reason that all these

minerals and things are worth a lot more than the price. I'm more valuable *on* that planet than I am here working as a clerk. Now what I propose—"

"Young man, I congratulate you!" said Murphy. "I envy your youth and prospects! Godspeed and bless you!" And he answered the phone.

An aide took Chuck back to the walk and let him reel home on his own steam. He couldn't afford, now, an airlift. He had eleven long years before him when he couldn't afford one. He was perfectly free to walk unless his shoes wore out—no provision having been made to replace them in this budget of eighty percent of pay. He was particularly cheered when the aide said, "Just to stiffen your resolution, and for no other reason than because Madman Murphy really likes you, you understand that this is no provisional contract. If you don't pay, we garnishee your pay for the period and keep the planet, too. That's the law and we're sorry for it. Now, God bless you and goodbye."

Chuck didn't need blessings as much as he needed help. It was going to be a very long and gruesome servitude.

As the months drifted off the calendar and became years, Chuck Lambert still had his literature to console him but nothing else. It is no wonder that he became a little lopsided about Planet 19453X.

He had a brochure which had one photograph in it and a mimeographed sheet full of adjectives, and if the photograph was not definitely of his planet and if the adjectives did not add into anything specific, they cheered him in his drudgery.

Earth, at this time, had a million or more planets at its disposal, several hundred thousand of them habitable and only a hundred and fifty colonized. The total revenue derived by Earth from these odds and ends of astronomy was not from the colonies but from the sale of land to colonists. The normal price of land on New World, being about one and one-half cents an acre, was a fair average price for all properly colonized planets. Unsurveyed orbs, nebulously labeled "Believed habitable," were scattered over the star charts like wheat in a granary.

On the normal, colonized planet, Earth's various companies maintained "stations" where supplies, a doctor and a government of sorts were available. On Planet 19453X there would be no doctor, no supplies, and no government except Chuck Lambert.

He realized this in his interminable evenings when he sat, dateless, surrounded by technical books, atlases and dirty teacups. The more he read of the difficulties overcome by the early colonizers on warrantedly habitable planets, the thinner his own project began to seem.

He would cheer himself at these times by the thought that the whole thing was only costing him twenty-five thousand dollars and blind himself to the fact that better-known bargains often went for two hundred fifty dollars on the government auction block. Chuck was top-heavy with imagination. He let it be his entire compass.

At the end of three years he had made a great deal of progress. The librarian had come to know him. She was a pleasant young thing who had her own share of imagination—and troubles—and it gave her pleasure to dredge up new books for Chuck to imbibe. Her guidance—her name was Isabel—and his voracity put him through medicine by the time four years had passed, electronics by five and a half, geology by six, mineralogy by seven, government theory by seven and a quarter, space navigation by eight, surveying by nine, and all the rest of the odds and ends by eleven.

She was rather good-looking, and when she had finally lost her first, elementary desire to marry a millionaire, she began to understand that she was in love with Chuck. After all, when you spend eleven years helping an ambitious young man to plow through a dream, you are likely to be interested in him.

She would have gone with him without another thought if he had asked her. But his last visit to the library was a very formal one. He was carrying a bouquet and he said a little speech.

"Isabel, I hope some day to prove a worthy investment of your time. I hope to be able to bring you a three-headed butler or maybe a dog in a matchbox to show my appreciation of your interest. Tomorrow I am faring forth. Goodbye."

This was all with some embarrassment. He wanted to ask her but he was afraid of her a little, libraries having that air.

She took the bouquet and suddenly realized she was liable to cry. She wanted to say something close and intimate, something to cheer him in his great adventure, something he could hold in his heart when the days and nights were lonely. But all she managed was a "thank you" because a child with a runny nose was clamoring to be heard on the subject of having lost his last book.

Chuck went away. When he reached the steps, and the moldy dignity of dead men's immortality no longer gripped him, he suddenly expanded. He was almost off on his great adventure. He would come back and lay a planet at her feet—or at least would invite her to one. He would catch her out of the library and propose to her and they would found a race of kings quite unlike the youngster with the runny nose.

He expanded and his dreams got bigger as he walked. He went down to the company and, with something of a grand air—spoiled a little because everyone was so busy—said that he was off tomorrow for Planet 19453X and glory. The girl gave him his time and asked him, after he had told her about his voyage, what his forwarding address would be. He started to explain that he was off for beyond beyond and would have gone far when he saw by her fixed, polite smile that she hadn't heard a word he said.

But there was still Murphy. In the morning when he came down to the office he expected his hand to be pumped, a bottle of champagne to be broken across his space helmet and ribbons to be cut. Instead he found a sallow-faced, bored clerk reading a racing form and the clerk had never heard of him. Madman Murphy never came in on Saturdays.

Chuck went into a passionate explanation and the clerk finally consented to look in the files. He did this with such a superior air that Chuck almost murdered him.

The contract was found, the payments were checked, the clerk was finally satisfied—if somewhat surprised, for the number of such that were finally paid out were quite few—and called a man named Joe to tell him that a Star-Jumper IV was to be placed at the disposal of one Chuck Lambert.

Chuck took his deed, checked the notary's commission, checked the description, checked the location and, in short, wore the clerk's patience entirely out. Finally Chuck took it and went to the registry office, which was closed.

The janitor, however, proved of aid and informed him that he could send it in by registered mail, retaining a photostat. Chuck thanked him and was not further balked, for a lithographer was near at hand and eager for business.

At the port, Chuck landed with his light luggage, left it under cover from the light drizzle which had begun, and went to find Joe. It took six searched hangars and a coffee shop to locate the greaseball and then it seemed that Joe had thought the ship was to be ready for Tuesday. However, much pressing got consent for today.

The next six hours were worse than the past eleven years. Chuck was here, so very near his goal, that seconds stretched out into light-years for him. What constituted his grand gesture was all muddled up and tangled with a number of details like Joe needing another cup of coffee and the starboard magnetrons being worn out on the Star-Jumper and having to be replaced and the hydraulic jack which wouldn't function and after an hour's repair had to be abandoned for another one which had stood right there all the time.

If Chuck had not got out of that port that afternoon he would have died of apoplexy, youth or no youth.

He was almost ready, the ship was finished, the port

clearance secured and Joe given a final cup of coffee, when he found out that the food supplies he had had shipped to the port could not be found.

It was dark, a rainy, wet dark, when he finally rose from the port, entered the acceleration height, put down his throttle and was gone. Chuck Lambert had never tasted such sweetness. The 4G sag was nothing to him. The age and obsolescence of the ship was nothing to him; his empty stomach was entirely forgotten. Here was sweetness. After eleven years he was on his way.

Now, inasmuch as the Sunday feature sections you see do such a fine job of telling how space travel looks and feels and as you may have done some of it yourself and so don't need to be told, a light-year-by-light-year description of Chuck Lambert's voyage to Planet 19453X is not necessary.

He saw the strange phenomena of light changes, size changes, star displacements and elongations and he felt all the bodily discomforts and euphorias and he saw the dark stars and luminous masses and, in short, he gloried in it. He wrote a log which sounded like a piece of poetry done by at least Julius Caesar. Space and the Universe were his onion. He ran out of dimensions like a spilled wineglass.

If he left anything out and if he missed anything, it was because after three or four days of it he had to get a little sleep.

He spent the following month filling his log, checking his course and building up a paper empire which stopped only because most of his supplies were not paper-wrapped and he ran out of writing materials.

Probably few men have ever owned as much conquered Universe and purchased earth as Chuck Lambert in those long weeks of his voyage. But all things must come to an end and all dreams must break. Chuck Lambert landed at last on Planet 19453X.

Now it happened that he had paid very little attention to his ship. The Star-Jumper was old and cranky and full of missing rivets. Her type had been developed for courier service in the first Colonial Revolt and about fifty thousand like her had been sold at a hundred dollars apiece to a man named Fleigal in Brooklyn. Her sole virtue was her near approach to perpetual motion, but of her drawbacks there is not enough paper here to adequately condemn them. Like any military job she had neither grace nor charm, safety nor comfort. And she managed this landing in a way calculated to drive any veteran of the spaceways entirely off his usual imbalance. She would not sit down.

Had Chuck been a more experienced navigator he still would not have understood why. And he was very far from that. When he reached the star, he had to brake to a full stop in the middle of the system and take five hours' worth of painful navigation to make sure the star was the right one. Then he used up two days examining orbits and the planets which ran in them to find 19453X, a thing which any professional would have finished up before he had the star itself within a light-year.

But the hunt-and-poke system at last gave results and Chuck, without observing at least one very strange fact about this area, tried to get down.

19453X had an atmosphere and a great many clouds. It was about seven times the size of Earth. It had no seas but seemed to possess a remarkable number of marshy areas which left the dry land at about one-fifth. It had numerous ranges of mountains and great, stretching plains. Chuck had all this down and noted with some enthusiasm, for it was his world, all his.

And then the Star-Jumper drifted somewhere between ground and sky, no power, no lifts, nothing.

Chuck became aware of this situation after a moment or two. The leaded ports were not such to permit a very good view below. He put a trifle of power to the magnetrons because he was anxious to get there.

He had his kingdom all organized and his palace half built when he touched and his head was full of such a confusion of thoughts that he was not instantly aware of anything wrong.

Then he unbuckled himself from the pilot's seat and started to get up. Two things happened. He hit his head on the overhead and the ship came off the ground.

He was not aware of the second fact until he opened the door to the rear compartment. He thought he must have left a throttle open and hastened back to the seat. His feet got no traction. No throttle was open. The Star-Jumper was going skyward at an amazing rate.

Chuck buckled himself in again and, with patience, put the ship down once more. He stayed there at the controls and watched, just in case. He was in a grottolike valley, honeycombed, colorful hills before him and beside him. These promptly began to recede once he shut the power off. He was rising!

Chuck was no electronic genius. He had read the books. And they didn't have any answers for this. He assumed a high wind and poured on power. Back went the ship, bump, bump against the ground.

He didn't want to bother about this anymore. He was too anxious to see his planet, stand on it, feel it and taste it. If his ship wouldn't stay landed, then there were ways to do it.

He coaxed the controls until the Star-Jumper skittered over the ground. A big cave opened up in the hill ahead and he resolutely put his ship's bulk into it. It was a tight squeeze and it didn't help the paint, but the Star-Jumper's eccentricity was foiled. Whether it would or no, now, it had to stay down.

Chuck got up. He put on his helmet, took down some extra oxygen cartridges, buckled on his flying belt and was prepared to explore. That he was having difficulty in here getting traction and bumping into things, he did not heed. He was space-dizzy already. He had been knocking around in this interior for so many weeks he couldn't register any difficulty. He didn't.

He opened his air lock, closed it behind him with commendable caution, opened the outer port and started to jump down.

But he didn't jump *down*. He went up and hit the cave roof with a clang, to cling there like a bat upside down and completely bewildered. He was walking wrong end to and getting traction like a fly and, personally, it didn't feel good.

He stood there, head down, thinking about it. Nothing in the numerous books Isabel had dug out for him had contained any such data as this. Carefully he walked toward the light and came close to the opening. There he slipped and "fell" straight up over the lip and would have kept on going to the absolute zero of space if his flying belt hadn't been in working order. It was. About a thousand feet up, Chuck got it going and, with considerable gratification, power-dived back to his planet and by dint of some adjusting, made a soft landing in a clay bank, straight up.

The clay was very sticky and mired his boots considerably and, belt still going, he managed to clamber out of this strange bog to dry land. He tried here to turn his jets off and, much to his surprise, when he turned them off, he stayed right side up just as he thought he should.

Chuck heaved a very deep sigh of relief in that moment. For a while there he thought he had run into something which was way beyond his engineering depths; with some confidence now he struck out afoot for the first ridge which would let him over and into the broad valley he had spotted coming in.

Spaceports, being insulated the way they are, have a nasty knack of obscuring the view and he did not realize until he reached the crest that he had, indeed, a lovely, lovely planet.

It was green and purple and gold and the docks and rivers shined below him. Trees waved in a gentle wind, grass rippled, brooks laughed. It was charming.

It was green and purple and gold and the docks and rivers shined below him. Trees waved in a gentle wind, grass rippled, brooks laughed. It was charming.

He went down the slope, careful because he didn't seem to be able to restrain a bounding tendency he had never before noticed in his walk, and knelt reverently beside the first brook. It was his, all his.

Incautiously he started to remove his helmet, being all unguarded before this greenery, and promptly began to suffocate. It was not the pressure. As far as pressure went, that was about equal. It was the quality of the air. As soon as he started to breathe it he started to suffocate. He had enough promptitude to clamp his helmet back on and give himself oxygen and only that saved his life.

Was it because the air was poison? But no, he didn't seem to be poisoned, only unsatisfied. He stood there and blinked in the bright daylight at the lovely trees.

He looked at the brook. The water was laughing, but was it laughing at him? He scooped some up in his fingers, half expecting it to turn into vitriol, but it was cool and moist and pleasant. He opened his helmet air lock and inserted a cup of it, and when he got it through and got the swallow down he was instantly sorry. It came right back up.

It wasn't that it tasted bad; that would be a relief. It just wasn't the sort of thing his stomach wanted and his stomach didn't know why.

This made Chuck a trifle bitter.

A pretty brook, lovely clouds, obvious air. He made a hurried recheck of his oxygen supply and decided he had enough for a couple of months if he was careful of it. But what of his lovely kingdom?

He did not see that he had real live subjects until he had gone nearly a kilometer and then he saw the cluster of huts, neatly blended into a river bend's trees.

The village probably contained a couple of hundred people or things and Chuck instantly loosened up his gun in its holster and went forward quietly. But if he had just now seen them, they had long since seen him and there wasn't so much as a pet in that village.

He looked it over. Comical huts, fitted with round thatch roofs, floored with river reeds. There were metal cooking pots and metal weapons. And a real, live fire smoldered in the middle of the main hut. It was common. It was almost uninteresting except that these beings were sentient and skilled in a certain culture.

Perhaps he would not have had any intercourse with them at all if he had not, just as he was leaving, found the old woman.

She was too old to be spry and she was too scared to hide all of her in the hay pile and so Chuck tapped her gently and coaxed her out.

"Oof! Oof!" she screamed, meaning "Don't kill me!"

Chuck looked her over. The features were not quite right but this creature was a biped, looked remarkably like Earth women and certainly didn't offer him any menace.

Chuck made her understand, amid many "oofs," that nothing untoward was intended. His efforts to communicate the facts by signs, that he was the owner of this planet and that these people were his subjects were received round-eyed and interpreted in some outlandish fashion he was never to know.

After a while she finally took him to the village center

where a bucket of water stood beside a big stone square and Chuck sat down. He knew he couldn't drink the water but he wanted to appear mild and tractable, the way a true planet owner should.

She went off and yelled around in the reeds and after some time a number of men, hairy fellows, mostly forehead and biceps, came back, carefully extending their spears to be ready to repel boarders, and finally saw that Chuck sat there mildly enough.

This was all very satisfying to Chuck. This was the way it should be. They considered him a superior being and he began with many "oofs" to convince them how very safe and mild he was and how they would benefit from his rule. They got rather near and finally relaxed enough to ground their spear butts. Chuck grew expansive. He was talking through his electronic speaker, which was turned up rather high, and his voice must have reached a good long ways, for more and more people came curiously to see what was happening.

Finally a young maiden whom Chuck found not at all ugly crept forward and touched his foot. This excited some wonder. She looked bravely up at him and he felt elevated. She took a stick and began to clean the clay off his boots with short pries and Chuck, in middle sentence, found himself getting lighter and lighter. He was a foot off the ground before the end of his uncomprehended paragraph and was beginning to accelerate when his audience took off with one long scream of alarm.

The girl crouched where she had been, looking up. Chuck rose to a hundred feet, going faster, got his jets going at last and came down.

The girl crouched where she had been, looking up.
Chuck rose to a hundred feet, going faster,
got his jets going at last and came down.

The girl cringed, head bowed, shivering. Chuck touched her hair and then a jet spluttered and he went up once more. Altogether he considered the interview at an entire end. Humiliated, he navigated himself over the center of the village, looked sadly down at the frightened eyes peering from the reeds and then changed his course back to the ship. Enough was enough for one day.

He sat for a long time on his cabin ceiling, thinking about fate that night. He wrote a letter to Isabel in which he confessed himself entirely confounded and disheartened. Before he finished it he was beginning to get mad at Madman Murphy.

Eleven years. Eleven hard, toilsome years for a planet he couldn't even walk upon!

He crept out about midnight and looked at the stars, holding on hard to the cave lip to keep from flying away into space, and then it occurred to him that he had a legal course.

He went back to it and worked it out. It was true. He was on the extreme perimeter of the galaxy. The star in whose system his planet lay was not, contrary to ordinary behavior, traveling outwards from the hub but was traveling inwards at a fast rate. Elementary calculation showed that it was making some thousand miles a second into the galaxy. If he could claim that this was not, as the contract stated, a system belonging to the Earth Galaxy, then he could have Madman up before the courts and have his money back. With that he could buy another place, a few thousand acres on some proven colonial orb, and he and Isabel could settle down and raise kids. And then he got to thinking about the vagaries of law and the money lawyers cost and realized that Madman Murphy would never have to refund a penny.

This almost crushed him.

He had a planet on which he could not possibly live, whose air he could not breathe, whose water he could not drink, and the owning of it had taken the best of his life. He was almost ready to end it all when he heard a rustling outside.

There was a *clink-clink.*

Visions of a combat, blaster against spears, drove all thought of suicide away and he helmeted himself promptly and passed through his air lock to find, not warriors, but the girl who had cleaned his boots.

It was hard standing on the ceiling shining a light down upon her. She was very humble. She had a bowl of white liquid which was probably milk and a little piece of bread and she made shivery motions at them.

Instantly Chuck knew he was a god.

Now there have been many men in the human race who have found themselves gods and never once has it failed to bolster their drooping spirits nor spur their lagging wits. She had come like a brave little thing to leave food for the goblin and if she died in the consequence, she had done it all for her village. It was plain.

Chuck hand-holded down his ship side and came near her. He knew better than to try to eat that food and it wasn't food he was interested in. It was the fact that she walked on the ground and he couldn't. She had some beads around her neck, metal spheres of some brilliance. He held his hand for them and she took them off and gave them to him. He gave her a fountain pen which had ceased to work and when she accidentally let it go, he brought it down from the ceiling and returned it to her. She tied it with a dress string and there it bobbed, trying to rise.

"Oof, oof," she said, meaning "Thank you."

"Thank you," Chuck said, meaning "Oof, oof."

He remembered, as he looked at these beads, the clay on his boots and he swiftly put several handfuls of rocks in his pockets. They kept him down. This was nerving. He went for a walk with her in the starlight.

It is certain they did not talk about much. It is also certain that Chuck did a terrible lot of thinking. He did a lot of calculating in an elementary way and then, suddenly, things came right to him.

Madman Murphy had skunked him. There was no recourse. But it had been an adventure.

He was taking her back to the ridge so that she could descend to her valley and tell people it wasn't so tough talking with gods after all and that they did not always go spinning off into space on you. But just before they reached the place he would leave her she stopped and pointed into a hole in the hill.

There were lots of holes in the hill but she was insistent about this one as one of the local sights and he obliged her and startled her into a screech by turning on a flashlight and shining it down.

He almost screeched himself.

The whole hole was glittering yellow.

Chuck went wonderingly forward and put out a gingerish hand. The entire place was studded with pure metal. Pure yellow metal. Where ore came in veins on Earth, it came in solid elements up here. As far as he could estimate he was looking, down this tunnel centuries old, at about a thousand million tons of metal.

This was what they made into spears and vessels, and he had missed the quality of these items only because spears and vessels get dirty. He was afraid to examine it closer. He could see from where he was that if there was this much in one hole . . .

Chuck took a piece and tested it. But it was very hard. He pounded at it a bit. It was still too hard. He looked at it and let it fall. He put a knife into a crack and tried to pry out a bigger piece and the knife slipped and went up and lay against the roof of the drift.

Chuck stood there and thought about it. Then he raced back to the ship, leaving the girl where she was, and returned carrying whatever was of weight he had been able to grab. He went to work.

Two months later, Chuck Lambert sat behind a big desk in the Universe Building in New York City.

The newspaper reporters even were awed by the proportions of this office and the scientists and businessmen present were very polite.

Chuck had his feet up and sat mostly on the back of his neck.

"Boys," he said, "you've got all the story there. How I made the trip, what I found, what I intend to do. I think that's about it."

"Mr. Lambert," said a *Ledger* reporter politely, "as a matter of human interest, could you let me have some personal details. Some little thing— You mentioned a girl named Isabel—"

"Married," said Chuck. "Married yesterday up at the City Hall. That's why," he added with a big grin, "I don't want to drag on here."

"But this girl on 19453X—" said another reporter.

"Rich. She'll be richer. They'll all be rich even if I don't ever see my subjects again. Now if you don't mind—"

"Mr. Lambert," said the business manager of International Flyways, "you are sure you can deliver enough of this material—"

"Enough," chimed in Ross of Ross Construction, "to make skyscrapers—"

"And bridges—" added the bridge builder.

"And spaceships," said Intercolonial's man.

"Gentlemen," said Chuck, "I towed down a piece of that metal as big as the village men could hack out and melt up for me. That was with crude stuff. Just a sample. I've got billions, billions of cubic yards of it and no cost to transport. It's cheap and since I filed on the rest of the planets in that system, I'm afraid this is a monopoly. But just the same, the price is the same as steel to you. Now if you don't mind—"

They were satisfied and they filed out, all but one thick-lensed little man.

"Mr. Lambert, I know you are in a hurry, being new-married and all, but I was so far in the back—"

Chuck beamed on him. The little man took heart.

"I'm from *Daily Topics,* you know," said the little man. "Our readers . . . well, they like to get a pretty lucid account—"

"Sure," said Chuck. "Sure." He waved a hand at the glittering nodules of metal on his desk which were encased in lead holders. He took one out and it promptly lifted and went up to the ceiling where it stuck. Chuck, after a few jumps, got it down again.

"That's Lambert metal for you," said Chuck. "Floats. Rises. Negative weight. Point nine-tenths the tensile strength of steel. Can be forged—"

"But I don't understand what makes it rise," pleaded the little man.

"Planet 19453X—which I have rechristened Isabel—is part of a renegade system which moved in from another galaxy after some interminable crossing of space. It is traveling toward our hub but it won't get there for another three or four billion years. Its matter is made of another kind of energy from ours, which, making up in usual atomic and molecular forms, has no affinity or repulsion for our own matter. It is very simple. It just isn't made of the same kind of energy."

"But what makes it rise?"

"Planets revolve and things on their surface have centrifugal force. This material still has mass, and so it seeks to rise. Therefore it will make bridges which need no abutments, ships which have to be cargoed to be kept in the atmosphere, skyscrapers which will have to be anchored, not founded—but I am sure you understand."

The little man blinked. He released one of the balls of Lambert metal and it went up to the ceiling. He fled.

Chuck Lambert went home to Isabel to plan out a ninety-room house on Long Island and five kids.

Madman Murphy has a big picture of Chuck in his window and a fine argument about wildcat planets. But don't trust him. There was only one 19453X.

The Conroy Diary

The Conroy Diary

IT is with considerable surprise that the researcher into ancient and forgotten lore first encounters the "Conroy Diary." Inevitably, if he neglects the foreword before perusing the text, he is startled by the flamboyant style, the indelicacy of the anecdotes and the altogether royal presence of mind of the redoubtable Conroy. He will look hurriedly for explanation in the beginning and find it.

"Dear reader," the foreword of any original edition will say. "Do not be too amazed by the brilliant exploits of our dashing hero. Conroy, alas, lives only in the mind of Fitz Mallory, his creator, and any resemblance to persons, places and planets is purely extraordinary and probably fortuitous."

It is well that the diary so begins. It was a work of fiction written by one of the most remarkable characters Earth ever produced, the fabulous Fitz Mallory.

In a day when adventure languished and the life of man seemed trite, Fitz Mallory came upon the scene as a God-given boon to mankind. He made an entire generation rock with laughter and gape with amazement, and what is far more important, Fitz Mallory sold the idea of space conquest to the human race.

Mallory's inevitable good fortune was something of a

legend. He was a man of inexhaustible resources, material or mental, and he lavished both upon his race with a hand so prodigal that, once, he nearly wrecked the economy of the United States, a nation of the original Earth.

Since Mallory's time our race has produced richer and more powerful men, gaudier or more important figures. But none of these people ranked him in the service he performed. In the ensuing hundred thousand years people still recalled Mallory even when they had forgotten his book.

"Conroy's Diary" makes wild sport of every accomplishment known to man and it particularly plays the buffoon about space travel. To quote it is no purpose here for it can be found rather easily in the libraries of any major galaxy. To tell the story of Fitz Mallory is the thing which needs to be done. He was not, as so many school children seem to believe, a god of an ancient mythology. He was a flesh-and-blood man. Crowned, perhaps, with more than his share of luck and wit, he still had his mortality. His tomb in the Earth National Park is a popular shrine and few days pass when fresh flowers or wreaths are not hung about it by some individual or organization. It is surmounted by a statue of Mallory, life-size, garbed in the space gear of that time, his head back in a magnificent laugh. The several times it has been restored have distorted the features a trifle. The garments are a bit chipped, but the laugh is still there. He is indeed Fitz Mallory, Crown Prince of Space.

In piecing together this remarkable man's life, the historian is quickly struck by the absence of actual facts. So coated, buttered and floodlighted is the reputation that to discover the man under it is difficult.

He seems to have begun his career in an orphan's home and the record appears to be entirely innocent of proper schooling. But there were not and are not schools to teach what Mallory had to learn.

At ten he was with Krinsky on the Pluto Expedition. Just how he got there is obscure but the logs of Krinsky carry continual mention of a mascot he calls Mr. Luck and it can be assumed that this was Mallory. According to these records and the news stories of the expedition, the fifty-man company found itself to be fifty-one the first day out or, as Krinsky says, fifty and a half.

If he did anything on Pluto, Mallory himself never seems to have mentioned it. But it was one of those fortunate expeditions which sail smoothly along a careful plan and all fifty and a half returned.

At fourteen Mallory deserted civilization again in favor of the Roberts Rescue Expedition which took the bodies of the ill-fated *Lombard* off Saturn. The sight of the bodies does not appear to have damped Mallory any, for at seventeen he is to be found aboard the *Golden Lion* on the Mars run as second mate, or so the shipping records of the day declare.

It is remarkable that, with all this data from which to draw, Mallory never wrote a line about the Solar System. And it was equally remarkable that he signed off the *Golden Lion* when he was eighteen and did not again appear in any record until he was thirty-one.

Then Mallory becomes, suddenly, Mallory the great, the darling of Earth. He wrote a book. It was about the mythical adventures of an outrageous man named Conroy and it was rapidly banned by all societies for the prevention of vice. The book was about a hundred thousand words in length and it purported to tour one Conroy on several voyages to various star systems wherein he dueled with dragons and got drunk with the daughters of humanoid kings and was deified or jailed as the popular whim might dictate. But whatever happened to Conroy, he was always the victor, always the hero, always loaded with the favors of damsel and king and Conroy always said so.

The book came after two government expeditions had gone out to Alpha Centauri and found humanoids. Their reports sounded so ridiculous and the work itself was so comparatively useless that Man was in a mood to laugh. And at that psychological moment, in stepped Fitz Mallory's "Conroy" and Mankind roared with mirth.

According to the memoirs of a Captain Sauvage, the Explorers Club was officially stern but unofficially very amused.

Sven Durlinger came there, one quiet Sunday afternoon, on a search for Mallory and he found him.

Mallory was a big man, very good to look upon, tawny haired and strong. He had a group of thirty or forty members and guests hanging on his words, already laughed into exhaustion and ready to laugh more.

"But how," pleaded a young man, "did Conroy ever get out of the dungeon?"

But whatever happened to Conroy, he was always the victor,
always the hero, always loaded with the favors of
damsel and king and Conroy always said so.

"There's no law against kings having daughters, is there?" boomed Mallory. "And while it is true that she had three heads, Conroy knew instantly that three heads are better than one and . . . hello, Sven!"

"Hello, Fitz," said Durlinger. He was a small man, the navigator and chief pilot of the Allied Survey Expeditions. "Don't let me interrupt you."

"Not at all! Come over here and have a drink. Boy, go find Mr. Durlinger a drink. I heard you've been looking for me."

Sven nodded. "It's kind of public here."

"Fire away!" boomed Mallory. "I have nothing to conceal. I hope."

"Well," began Sven diffidently, "it's kind of trying to come back after a year spent in a vacuum to find the whole world laughing about space travel."

"Now, Sven. You're not mad."

"No. I guess not. But it's upsetting. We worked like the devil around Alpha Centauri. And we didn't get out of any dungeons with the help of the king's daughter, either. I thought you were a friend of ours."

"I am. I am!"

"Mallory, you've put back space travel fifty years. Every new thing that comes in, somebody will snort and say that Conroy should have found it. It's very difficult to bring people to realize just what a spanking big Universe that is out there and how many various things there are in it. They were laughing already without the help from your Conroy. We have a flying dog—"

The whole crowd laughed. Sven shrugged. "You see. Even

34

you salty characters are ready to classify straight out of that confounded diary. We really do have a flying dog. Space exploration is serious stuff, Fitz."

"Drink up," said Mallory. "It will make you feel better."

"When you and I were with Blanding on the *Golden Lion,* you were dead serious about all this. You yourself said one night that Man's only salvation lay in the stars. Why kill it?"

"Sven," said Mallory, "just what did your expeditions prove that hadn't been proved already? Nobody on the whole planet is going to sail off and stake out a homestead on Lincoln of Alpha Centauri. We have our fun, let them have theirs."

"Speaking of fun," said Sven, "where *have* you been in the last ten years? You don't seem very out at elbows. Or is that the book paying royalties?"

"Well, as for that," said Mallory, "I got me a small loan from Conroy."

They all laughed and when Mallory had told them just how Conroy had got the capital which furnished the source of that loan, they laughed harder. It had to do with selling a necktie, which lighted up, to a certain medicine man on some weird planet of which no one had ever heard. Then Mallory took Sven out of there.

They rode uptown to Mallory's apartment and there they found the butler waiting and the cook with dinner ready. Sven stood around and blinked. This apartment must be worth two or three thousand a month and the furniture was capable of paying a few ransoms. Did books make this much money?

Sven mellowed out a bit under the wine and what passed

between them at the table is no matter of record. Sven went away the next day and was not seen again for an entire year.

But whatever happened to Sven Durlinger, it could not bother Fitz Mallory. Nothing ever bothered him. He went on his princely way, attending levees, autographing books, smiling on old ladies and young children and spending lavishly far beyond whatever his means could have been.

At the Museum of Natural History in New York, Earth, there is a copy of a speech made by Mallory on the occasion of opening a new wing. They did not intend to have Mallory speak, for the occasion was solemn. There was to be a new exhibit of fauna and flora from Lincoln, Alpha Centauri and there were many additions to the Mars-Venus displays.

The Curator of Other Worlds was astonished to read in the morning press that this afternoon Fitz Mallory was to speak there. Ordinarily he would have instantly protested but it happened that he knew Mallory and one does not usually offend men who are six feet four. He held his peace. At two o'clock he was doubly astonished. The hall, which held four thousand, was packed and people were piling up in the streets. This dazed him. A five hundred person attendance would have been remarkable.

He was wringing futile hands and wondering about the courtesy of turning so many away when a rigging truck drew up and eight communications men plunged through the crowd which was piling up in the street to install a dozen speakers and a huge visio screen so that the overflow could see and hear if it filled the entire park.

It did fill the park. Mallory came, leading a strange looking animal with six legs, a huge head and horns about twelve feet long. Mallory solemnly led the brilliant pink beast into the hall amid thundering cheers.

The curator made his pathetic little address about his new hall and then helplessly introduced Mallory.

There ensued a rapid-fire, booming lecture, a solemn-voiced atrocity of hashed up Latin and mangled zoology in which Mallory exhibited the curator by mistake as a specimen taken on the planet Jungo-Boola of the System Gastric, caught after three hundred humanoid beaters had lost their lives. Mallory recognized his error and humbly apologized and then absent-mindedly began a flora speech on a potted palm which had been on the platform there since time had begun. Its deadly poison was the result of a malevolent eye which grew in the center of the tree, he said, and the already laughter-weakened audience shrieked when the president of the museum rose with haughtiness from his seat behind that palm.

The *pièce de résistance*, however, was the six-legged alihipidile from far-off Bingo-Bocbum of the Roulette System. This ferocious beast used its horns to spear doughnuts and lived on a diet of mink coats which made it expensive to keep. However, for the benefit of the assembled, Conroy himself had brought this beast all the way from far-off Bocbum at great and terrible expense and only that morning had had to take donations on Fifth Avenue to make up a proper ration. If any showgirls were in the crowd . . . But at this point the six-legged alihipidile revolted and began to buck and suddenly came apart into three men and a hide which caused such obvious embarrassment to Fitz Mallory, who reviled the absent Conroy, that it broke up the show.

About a month later the Geophysical Society found that it had scheduled a meeting it did not know about when the curious members attended Carnegie Hall which had been rented for the night, admission free. They were stunned at the vastness of the apparatus strung about the stage. They did not understand anything about this until Fitz Mallory, tawny and laughing, came upon the stage and greeted a packed hall with the news that tonight he was going to show them the newest inventions for space travel.

There proceeded a display of scientific mumbo jumbo which made the audience scream and the Geophysical Society squirm. Folding spittoons, self-disposing rations which did not have to be eaten, a flamboyantly introduced new ship heating unit which turned out to be a slinky brunette and other items rapidly reduced the sanity of the crowd. And then Fitz Mallory demonstrated the newest and greatest invention of all. It was a gravity shield, he said. And he slid a piece of the material under him. Promptly he began to drift off the floor, noticing the fact so late that he had a terrible time shifting over to get down again. As he lectured he absent-mindedly kept stepping on the shield and rising and finally, as his lecture reached its climax, stumbled across it and promptly soared straight up and out of sight. A few seconds later he was coming down again but he was angrily arguing with the man in the wings who was working a reel and fighting to get loose from the wires which were harnessed to his coat.

It ended the breath of the audience and the show.

But although the publishers of the book were delighted with these things, the scientific world was not. Fitz Mallory had stepped too far when he had billed Carnegie Hall as he did. He was thrown bodily out of the Geophysical Society. The Explorers Club was far too tolerant to take action but it became cool.

The Society for the Exploitation of Space, very old now and staid, struck Mallory from its list and recommended that the government take some action. The government did take action, but not of the expected kind.

For a year Fitz Mallory had been spending money. And he had made no income tax return. Conroy, romping through further adventures in a second book, had obviously brought in more money than the publishers reported having paid Mallory.

Two investigators, working quietly, found that Mallory had spent, one way or another, something more than a million dollars during the year. They had the facts and, shortly, they had Fitz Mallory.

They interviewed him politely in the Collector's Office—politely as befitted a man who must owe them a million and probably more.

It was the third of May of that memorable year. There had been murders and robberies and a senator slain in a love nest but the headlines all talked about Fitz Mallory and the government.

"WORLD'S GREATEST LIAR BAFFLING GOVERNMENT" is a sample of these scareheads. If war had been declared, no greater stir would have been made. Everybody waited to hear about this one. The papers repeated past exploits, including the latest, a fiasco wherein Fitz had been exhibiting the largest dwarf ever caught on Flub-Mub of the Sambo System, a person some eight feet tall, known to anyone who had ever seen a jungle motion picture as Sam Casper of Sioux Falls.

"Mr. Mallory," said the collector, "you must have some accounts of your transactions and some explanation of your income."

Fitz sat back and counted thoughtfully on his fingers. He made some secret figures on a piece of paper and destroyed it. He pulled out a slide rule and slaved over it. Then he drew out a pocket adding machine and worked with it for ten breathless minutes.

Finally he said, "Nope."

The collector was stern. "Mr. Mallory, I must warn you that unless you divulge your sources and explain yourself satisfactorily, we are prepared to send you to prison."

"On what evidence?"

"We have received secret information from an anonymous but identifiable source to the effect that your income during the past year was more than a million dollars. All but twenty-nine thousand of that is, of course, tax."

"A secret informer?"

"Yes, that is the case. I have the affidavit here."

Mallory seemed to deflate. He looked very sad. "I shall have to get my books. It will take me almost a week. You won't send me to prison, will you?"

"Unless you pay, frankly I have no choice."

Fitz went out and found the street jammed. Cameras flashed, people cheered. Reporters tried to learn something.

Mallory pulled out a tin cup and a pair of dark glasses and sat down on the steps, putting up a sign, "I got to pay a tax. Please help the needy. Conroy is out of town."

During the week Fitz made several volunteer lectures on the fauna and flora of the Treasury Department. He offered land for sale on the Planet Slumgo of the Blue Sky System—a billion acres of it at ten dollars an acre. He had an atmosphere ship paint a huge sign over New York, "S O S Conroy. All is forgiven. Come home. Mallory. P.S. I need a million dollars." This was in reverse as it would be addressed to some star.

Meantime the press kept asking, "WILL MALLORY GO TO JAIL?"

And the Collector of Internal Revenue kept replying, "Yes. Unless . . ."

The week was finally at end. Fitz Mallory delivered himself up.

Solemnly he placed a dozen ledgers on the desk of the collector and sank wearily down. Reporters had been admitted at Mallory's request.

"This is no sideshow," warned the collector. "I am sick of this buffoonery. I do not care a straw about popular opinion. I am doing my job as I have been ordered to do it and I have no other choice." This, delivered to the reporters, was properly noted.

The collector approached the ledgers. He opened the first one. The top entry was, "Full price for the Planet Slumgo, $100,000." The next read, "Loan repaid to Moolamaun, King of the Tarkabs, $10, in beads." The following was, "Ransom of Miss Geeber, cut price, to her friends on Kaledon—price cut for certain considerations, $1,000,000. In diamonds."

The collector slammed the ledger to the floor. "I have been used long enough for publicity to sell books! These are no accounts. You have no sense of decency! Mr. Mallory, I cannot permit this to continue. Produce your sources of revenue—"

There was a slight commotion at the door and a man walked in. He was clad in a tattered spaceman's coat and belted about with a scratched stomach protector. He was unshaven and he was tired.

The collector glared at him for the intrusion. "And who the devil might you be?"

"I am Sven Durlinger, lately chief of the Recheck Expedition. This is my friend, Fitz Mallory. I understand that there is some trouble here about income."

"Trouble enough!" said the collector. "And enough that you needn't add more."

"Sir," said Sven quietly, "I can testify that Fitz Mallory's income from his books was bequeathed to various charities. I have seen the records and I know the charities."

"Who are you to testify that?" demanded the collector.

A small man in the rear of the room, an attorney for the publisher, came forth with an imposing book. On inspection it disclosed that not one penny of the sales of the "Conroy Diary," volumes one and two, had been given to Fitz Mallory.

This was curious enough. What followed was worse.

"Fitz Mallory," said Sven Durlinger, "is a firm believer in the future of man in space. He should be. He made enough money there." Sven turned to the reporters, "Gentlemen, Fitz Mallory is a fraud."

This was not news.

"He is a fraud," said Sven Durlinger, "because he has written the truth." He unrolled a long series of photographs and beckoned up a young space officer who had a pile of documents. They were strange photographs. They were stranger documents.

As the collector made his inspection, Sven continued. "Gentlemen, for the past year I have been retracking. I have visited twenty-three planets in various systems, all of them habitable, seventeen of them inhabited by humans or humanoids of which you already know something.

"You will not lightly disregard my word, gentlemen, nor my evidence. I have a twelve-man crew to back me in everything I say.

"Fitz Mallory is a fraud. He has visited every one of those planets. He gave some of them outrageous names and he treated them all to outrageous adventures. He is considered a god on a round dozen of those worlds and a mention of his name was enough to bring kings kneeling at my feet. He is a fraud, gentlemen, because he is masquerading. There before you, and look at him well, is Conroy!"

The stillness of the room attested that nobody was breathing. Not one eye-blink fanned the air. They gaped at Sven Durlinger.

"For ten years, in the old *Liberty III*, which was given him by the great Krinsky on that man's death, Fitz Mallory cruised space, plotting the way, mapping routes, inventing means. The 'Conroy Diary' is truth told with a flare. What man would have believed it as fact? Who believed in space travel? From ample evidence received on the ground, I am prepared to attest that the majority of adventures which befell the mythical Conroy actually happened to Fitz Mallory.

"It rocks your wits, I know, to understand that this man is no clown. He carried forward a complete plan to credit space travel to everyone. He returned here from his last voyage, resolved to counter the usual rebuff. He countered it with the diary. You have all read it I am sure. It is true, gentlemen. True as sunlight! And the ledger I see open there on the floor must be a true ledger. The third item I know for a fact. I am afraid, Mr. Collector, that you have the wrong man."

The collector was sputtering now. He finally managed: "But this is no rebuttal of my charges! What do I care—"

"Indeed, I am afraid it is," said Fitz Mallory with a big grin. "That money was made out in the stars. All of it. It is exterior income for I am no resident, being an international citizen. Excuse me, Sir," he said rising, "but when I sent out Sven, I had a mission to perform. I have used you harshly, I fear."

"But the affidavit!" cried the collector. "The affidavit!"

"I wrote it," said Sven. "And Fitz mailed it to you as a report on himself. We are only interested in one thing—space travel."

"There's a charge for that," said the collector. And then, suddenly looking at Fitz, "Say, wait—you mean those Conroy tales are all true? You mean a man can have adventures like that out in space?"

"I am afraid so," said Fitz. "It's a rough life but a merry one. I am leaving soon on my next voyage. I could use a man like you."

"Could you?" said the collector, pleased. "I'll go!"

The papers ran it as it was played. There was a raging hurricane of argument throughout the world in the next few days. Fitz Mallory was discussed in half a hundred languages.

The world was laughing at itself. And it was laughing with Fitz Mallory, the god of a dozen habitable worlds, the owner of stars, the Crown Prince of Space.

He never wrote another book. He did not have to. He went away soon after to plot more routes.

They brought back his body some thirty-two years later. He had landed on one too many planets as all spacemen did sooner or later. They built him a big tomb and a famous sculptor made a statue of him with the most imperishable materials at hand.

Fitz Mallory still stands in gray obsidian, surrounded by flowers and offerings even today. His head is thrown back in a huge laugh and the legend on the base states:

> Fitz Mallory. God of a Hundred Worlds.
> He opened the Universe to Mankind.

The Planet Makers

The Planet Makers

DOYLE shook an outraged finger under the engineer's nose. "McGee, do I have to remind you that this entire job is to be finished in the next thirty days and you have barely started in four months?"

"Sleepy" McGee sat where he was, heels cocked up on an explosives box, his soles toward the construction hut stove. He had a visograph planted on another box with a cleared space before it, and in his hands he held a pack of cards. Sleepy McGee, of Planetary Engineering Construction Co., Inc., almost never got excited. He did not get excited now.

"My contract," cried Doyle, "calls for a bonus of a million dollars to your company for every day short of the promised time! But let me remind you that a penalty of one million dollars is to be paid to me for every day this job exceeds the specified time. Unless you quit this . . . this idle, supine—"

Doyle was fat. He was easily excited. His color was red and his cheeks were bellowing in and out.

"Mr. Doyle," said Sleepy, "have a drink."

Doyle's blood pressure would have broken a gauge. He turned and slammed into the air lock and was gone out into the methane-ammonia atmosphere of Alpha Jetabo's Planet Six.

Sleepy dealt the cards. He dealt them in such a way that they were visible to the visograph, all except his hole card, for this was stud poker. There is nothing peculiar in the playing of stud poker, but this game was with Mart Lonegan who happened to be on an engineering job of his own ninety-three light-years away. They had not seen each other for five years, face to face, but Mart owed Sleepy McGee nineteen-thousand-odd dollars to date.

Mart grinned on the visograph. "Was that Colonial Enterprises?"

"Yep," said Sleepy. "What you bet?"

"One white. Hold up my hole card again and don't look at it, you pirate, or I'll— Make that two whites."

Sleepy called and dealt the next cards.

"You're no closer than he says?" said Mart.

"Nope."

"*Wheeew!* That's a big planet, too."

"Ten thousand kilometers diameter," said Sleepy. "Your queen bets."

Barteber, the huge black cook, stirred stew over the camp range and stole an occasional peek when Sleepy raised his hole card. Barteber had been with Sleepy for nine years, one planet or another.

Mart Lonegan never found out that Barteber's silent whistles of surprise or glum looks—which Mart could see beyond Sleepy—meant absolutely nothing and were in reality a solid part of Sleepy's poker. Barteber would have given his right arm before he would have cost Sleepy a pot by betrayal, but Mart, being a trusting soul, did not know that.

Sleepy yawned. He was about six feet six and he had little weight to go with it, no matter his huge appetite. He drew fifty thousand dollars a year as a field engineer for Planetary Engineering Construction Co., Inc., and he dressed something worse than any one of his cat men. It was said of him in certain unsavory places in the universe that he could drink more liquor, play better poker, shoot with less compunction and yawn wider than any spaceman alive. That was exaggeration. He had met a man on Pilos who could play poker just as good.

The air lock whistled and slammed shut and Tommer Kaltenborn came into the construction shack, tugging off his helmet. Tommer was excited. He was a very young engineer, Tommer. He had come up as junior assistant to Planet Six as a replacement for a man who had carelessly tried to smoke inside his helmet, and Tommer recognized that he was having his chance and recognized, too, that he had ample opportunity to make it good.

No single school practice which Tommer had been taught was being followed on Planet Six. This was upsetting. It made his black hair stand up bristly straight and made his spectacle-rimmed eyes squint with disdain. If Sleepy McGee was an example of Planetary men, Tommer knew that one Kaltenborn would go far, very far.

"Number Eighteen cat's been sabotaged," said Tommer. "That's the fifth example of tampering since we got here. You've got to come out. The link pins are gone on the right tread. That leaves us just five cats. How we're to smooth down whole mountain ranges with five cats—"

Sleepy didn't have to look up. He knew what Tommer

looked like. He knew what the construction hut looked like. He said, "Hello, Tommer. Glad you came in. This visograph reception is bad. Very bad." He yawned. "We got any spiderwork steel left?"

"Sir, that cat—"

"How much we got?"

"About ninety kilos."

Sleepy squinted unseeing at his cards. "Hmmm. Well, run me up a twenty-thousand-foot tower outside here and put an aerial on it. And while you're about it, you might as well put one up on the opposite side of this chunk of mud. Put in a relay."

"Sir, Number Eighteen cat—"

"Run it in a hole and shovel dirt on it," said Sleepy. "Tell Maloney I want the towers done by daylight. When Mart deals, I can't tell a spade from a club."

Tommer glared. Resolutely, he put on his helmet, looked his contempt for a moment, and turned back into the air lock.

Barteber sniggered and Sleepy called the poker hand. Mart was found to be trying to make two jacks look like three.

Reception was really bad now and Sleepy knocked off the game. He got up, poured himself a neat slug of Old Space Ranger, handed the bottle to Barteber who, truth told, liked vanilla extract better, and got himself into a suit.

"That Mister Tommer, he want your job purty bad," said Barteber.

"He can have it," said Sleepy.

"And that Mister Doyle, he just plain froths. I never hear such a bloodthirsty man. You look out, Mister Sleepy."

"They aren't so dangerous."

"Well, just the same, I got a couple voodoo charms and a wax figger," said Barteber, and made a vicious attack on the stew.

Sleepy went out into the twilight of Alpha Jetabo's Planet Six. The place would be named New Eden when Colonial Enterprises took it over. They had it on lease from the Tronmane Confederacy. Sleepy looked at the distant mountain range, all rock and corners, and sighed. Certainly it was true that they had not made much progress in the four months they had been here. The one valley was about completed, which left a few billion square kilometers untended. It also left water and soil and air.

The planet was smaller than Earth but had a similar gravity. It would be a mono-season job, with an equatorial temperature of about ninety average. Its year was about one and a half Earth's, and outside of the blue character of Jetabo's Planet Six would not look too bad when it was finished.

They were burying the cat as ordered and an inertia ship was taking off with a cargo of spider steel to erect the opposite pole tower. Tommer was standing on a pile of new rock looking at a blueprint.

It was a pretty blueprint, being a Mercator with seas and rivers designated by flamboyant names. It was the prospectus blueprint of the Colonial Enterprises advertising division, and while it sold plenty of property it was not a very good guide for engineering.

However, that was nothing to Tommer. The job was contracted to be this way, and this way it would be. A contractor's first duty was to his builder.

Sleepy looked at the blueprint. "Honeymoon Bay," he said, pointing. This amused him. "Bide-a-wee Valley. They always get dopey ideas like this, kid. Don't take it so much to heart."

Tommer glared through lenses and helmet, and said, "We haven't even begun to construct these things. If we had been more on the job we would have found the saboteur and we would still have what equipment we need. A thousand kilos of powder blown up, twenty million feet of cable ruined, and now most of our cats out of commission. We'll never finish. This will bankrupt the company!"

"Well, kid," said Sleepy, "if you go on worrying like that you'll get ulcers. And when you have ulcers you can't drink. And when you can't drink you can't stand places like Planet Six, and there goes your career. Come over here and get somebody to drill me some holes."

They had the tower up, well pinned into the native rock, in about two hours. Sleepy looked admiringly up at this giddy spire into the methane clouds.

"I guess that'll do it," he said. "That reception was getting so darned bad that Mart won five pots today. When they get the other one—"

Maloney, straw boss of the dirt gangs, interrupted him. "You mean we been puttin' this thing up just so you could play poker with that crazy Lonegan?"

Sleepy yawned and smiled. "Well, Maloney, when you get as old as I am—"

"I'm five times older than you and you know it! Somebody just hooked every fuse we've got. Unless you can invent one, we ain't got a single detonator in camp. Who the devil is doin' this? By golly, if I get my mitts—"

"Now, now," said Sleepy. "We'll invent something. It'd be two months before we could get a new order of anything up here."

"Two months!" cried Doyle, who had toiled perspiringly toward them over the rubble which had been a mountain range. "Two months! I'll have colonists here in thirty days! McGee, I insist we line up these men and interrogate them one by one. There's somebody in this camp who doesn't want this planet completed!"

"You interrogate one by one," said Sleepy, "and they'll quit two by two. These men are loyal. You'll have to find something else. Maybe a methane-metabolism goon or a lost race. You let me do the worrying, Doyle."

"But you aren't worrying!" cried Doyle. "I have to think of my company's reputation. Do you have any idea how much money is being tied up here?"

"Well," said Sleepy, considering, "if you figure this planet at a billion arable acres and the acres at two dollars apiece, I got some idea."

"But they're not arable yet!" cried Doyle.

And he swept a despairing hand across the twilight vista. Truly, it was an ugly sight. In the shrinkings and contortings of a new-made world, vast escarpments had been heaved up. In the bluish, ghastly light, the raw, soilless, plantless valleys and mountains were nightmare stuff.

"You'll never finish!" cried Doyle.

Sleepy shrugged. He turned around and went back into the construction shack and threw his helmet down.

Tommer went into the communications dome and sent a long, telltale message to Planetary Engineering Construction Co., Inc. Doyle, shortly afterward, poured a flood of grief into the ether on his own.

At eight-seventeen there was a loud flash and men poured from their quarters to find that the cable shed was a shambles with not one foot of their remaining cable in usable condition. They poked in the ruins and went to report to Sleepy. But he was snoring in his bunk and Barteber would not let him be disturbed.

In the morning, Sleepy McGee shoveled in twenty hot cakes, washed them down with a quart of milk, chased it with a brandy and was ready to face the day.

He found Maloney and Tommer sitting disconsolate on a pile of demolished scenery and pulled them into his wake. He found half a dozen welders and drew them some drawings on a piece of sheet metal and sent them on their business.

"I heard footsteps walking around last night," said Doyle, coming up.

"Footsteps most always do," said Sleepy.

"Are you trying to be nasty?"

Doyle, for all his fat, was a big man. Sleepy looked him over.

"Now that I come to think of it, yes," Sleepy answered finally. "We've been having a lot of hard luck on this job.

Some rival of yours, or ours, has slowed us down to a walk. You haven't made things any easier."

"I don't sit around all day and play poker and drink liquor!" Doyle snapped.

"I'm not dumb and I don't have dirty fingernails," said Sleepy.

"Are you being insulting?"

"I never mix words," said Sleepy. "I *am* being insulting. In a brief four-letter word—"

Doyle struck at him. It is very difficult to work or fight in a methane-ammonia suit, but the blow staggered Sleepy. He went down on one knee and stayed there, with the eye of every construction man upon him. Languidly he got to his feet.

Suddenly he grabbed Doyle, avoided a second blow, and pitched the Colonial man about ten feet. Doyle hit, and he started to get up, but Sleepy's boot sent him down again. Doyle tried to rise a second time. Sleepy let him get all the way to his feet and then, with a short one to the midriff, knocked him gasping.

"I'll get you for this!" Doyle wheezed. "I'll report you!"

"Not on my visograph!"

"I'll . . . I'll return to your company! This will cost you millions, do you hear?"

And Doyle got up and ran to the Colonial Enterprises ship in the valley. Sleepy watched him go, watched the ship take off, watched the weird glow of the wake after it was gone.

"He'll make a lot of trouble," said Tommer.

"Kid, I was born out of Calamity by Trouble. Any engineer is.

Maloney, put a strong seal on Mr. Doyle's hut and don't let anybody disturb it. We wouldn't want to be accused of stealing his clothes."

"He'll be back here in a month," said Tommer. "That ship isn't any freighter. And he may bring in the Space Police for assault." He looked at Sleepy. Brawling—it was uncouth, ungentlemanly.

"Be that as he will," said Sleepy. "Let's go to work."

The mystified welders were putting hulls under the huts and it took them a long time to understand that Sleepy wasn't entirely crazy. Every now and then one of them would come into the construction shack, see Sleepy playing poker, open his mouth to speak, remember Doyle and back out.

They passed two nights of double-shift construction, with guards posted against sabotage, and then Sleepy condescended to come out and inspect what Tommer had been overseeing.

Twelve huts were all on sledges, as though to be dragged away. The men, glad that the work was done, dragged themselves into their bunks and slept. Sleepy sent for the atomic electrician, a driller and a shooter.

They put a few tools into a thousand-mile-an-hour ground-scanner and disappeared in a cloud of country rock, leaving a worried Tommer to sit and twiddle his thumbs and wait for the message he thought would come from Planetary, relieving Sleepy.

For five days Sleepy and the three men were "whereabouts unknown," and then they returned, tired, hungry and dirty, parked the scanner and turned in.

The following morning Sleepy got up around about eleven,

yawning and stretching and making jokes with Barteber. Tommer was all disapproval.

"Where did you go?" said Tommer.

"Had to block in the oceans and rivers, didn't we?" said Sleepy, with a wink at Barteber. "Have a drink, kid?"

"I don't drink."

"Well, there's no harm in that, but I always say that a good engineer is a lot better a quart later. Why, you ought to hear some of the things I've planned when I had two quarts! One time I figured out a scheme to build a bridge from Mars to Jupiter and I would have done it too, only the sun kept getting in the way. You see, it would have radized the metal and nobody could have crossed.

"And then there was the asteroid assembly project," he continued. "I did that on a bottle and a half. You ball up all the asteroids of some busted planet and they catch fission and you've got a sun close to cold planets which revolve around the original sun and lights the—"

"I'm sure it is impractical," said Tommer.

"Mister Kaltenborn, if Mister Sleepy says it will work," said Barteber, "it *will* work. I seen him take—"

But Tommer had left in disgust.

About one o'clock, Sleepy called the men together and made them take loose tools and equipment into the twelve sledged huts. Then he ordered the men themselves into the huts. At three, he and the atomic electrician took a lonely stand on the "deck" of the construction hut.

Sleepy pulled out a bottle. "Here's how."

"How," said the electrician with a grin.

Sleepy put his boot on a plunger and pressed.

Suddenly the upper atmosphere of Planet Six began to glow in pulsing sheets. The glow spread and brightened until it blotted the daylight. A beating concussion was faintly felt on the ground and Sleepy braced himself against the outer wall. He gravely presented the bottle again.

"Here's how," he said.

The electrician grinned. "How," he said.

They wiped their mouths by scrubbing them into their fur collars. The electrician shoved down on the second plunger.

There was a growing roar and the ground began to shake harder and harder until the mountains reeled and danced under the pounding of the upper flashes.

Suddenly the rain came. It was torrential. A man without a helmet would have drowned in a moment. The great drops battered at the rocks and rebounded until the entire surface everywhere was a racing glaze of water, water which mirrored the upper flashes. In a few minutes the valley where the cats had worked so long was so full that all was covered from sight. In half an hour the sledges themselves had become boats and were floating.

The water was shocked and beaten by the repeated earthquakes, and the ranges of mountains, invisible through the downpour, suddenly displayed themselves by their gigantic flashes. They were exploding into volcanoes.

The twenty-thousand-foot tower, anchored by force rays, shook under the onslaught, bending and quivering but standing just the same.

Suddenly the upper atmosphere of Planet Six
began to glow in pulsing sheets.

Sleepy pushed the bottle inside his helmet trap, said "Here's how," and drank once more, handing it to the electrician.

"How!"

And the third plunger went down.

It was time to duck. The sledges were bobbing already. Shortly something else would hit them. Wind. The blow began to scream in earnest about seven, and it kept up ceaselessly for the next three days.

The sledges were protected by the volcanoes to some extent, but they were battered, nevertheless, by a hundred-mile-an-hour storm. What the speed of wind must have been five miles up, no one could calculate. What batterings the hills and mountains took was not subject to mere computation.

Like a million banshees cut loose all at the same time, the hurricane roared on and on. Now and again mountains belched. Again and again new chain reactions went off in the upper atmosphere. And the water rose and rose and the waves surged and beat.

Sleepy played no poker. The visograph was out of operation for the moment. He lay in his bunk and read an erudite treatise called "Shady Ladies" and sipped his whiskey thoughtfully. Whatever Tommer might be thinking about all this was no concern of one Sleepy McGee.

About nine o'clock the morning of the tenth day, Barteber shoved a cup of hot coffee into Sleepy's sleeping hand and said, "The rain's stopped."

That woke Sleepy. He went to the leaded glass port where somebody had written the names and addresses of a half a dozen faraway girls and wiped off the chalk smears. Indeed, the rain had stopped. But the hurricane wind continued.

Sleepy drank his coffee and let the gale blow itself out. At three that afternoon the waters were calm and settling and he stood on the deck of his sledge and waved to men coming out on theirs. All twelve had weathered the elements, being undentable and self-contained, but two had dragged their moorings and were about a mile farther on.

Lifting his helmet gingerly, Sleepy took a sniff at the air. It was good and he removed his helmet. Jetabo's bluish haze was not so blue now, being filtered through a mist, and the aspect of this planet was something to gratify Sleepy's heart.

The water was draining away in huge rivers. The wind, having eroded mightily against every protrusion, had provided enough silt to color the streams brown. There would be bottom land and soil.

The following morning, Sleepy went off in a scout ship they had dredged up and took a look at the planet. He flew at ninety thousand feet, with tracers taking down all necessary data of coastlines, prominent rivers and mountains.

The geology had changed enormously, due to some thirty pounds of plutonium, a crude explosive, injected into this planet's core. The rarefied atmosphere had broken down the component parts of methane and ammonia into something which could be breathed everywhere on the planet. There were enough seas to provide air saturation and guarantee rainfall, and enough deposits of eroded soil to make crops possible.

When he returned just after dark, he had a map of the planet as it now existed and he could send, by latitude and longitude, four other planes to scatter tons of various seeds.

When he had sent them he found Tommer recovering from a bad case of seasickness. Tommer was sitting by the galley stove being consoled by Barteber and trying to get warm.

Sleepy was about to add his condolences when a sputter of jets told of a landing spacecraft and visitors.

Doyle was in complete helmet and ammonia suit, as were the rest, and they were astonished to find a window open. Nervously, Doyle made a motion to close it, saw that Sleepy, Barteber and Tommer wore no helmets and gingerly removed his own.

"I got action," said Doyle. "I brought your vice-president in charge of construction and he has seen fit—"

"Hello, Bainsly," said Sleepy.

"Hello, Sleepy. What's up?"

"You're in time to inspect," said Sleepy. "But have a drink." He poured several tumblers full. "She's got a proper atmosphere, with plenty of water in the right places. She's got soil and the boys are out scattering seeds to hold it where it is, and I guess that is about that. We're nine days ahead of deadline so that's a nine million bonus."

Doyle didn't drink. "That's impossible! When I left here twenty-one days ago, nothing had been done. You worked for four months—"

"You mean we studied potentials for four months," said Sleepy.

"You could have done this in half the time!" Doyle raged. "I demand to know why you fooled around with those cats!"

"Come," said Sleepy, and moved his languid length out to the deck.

He took the others over to the hut which had been sealed on Doyle's departure and had the seal struck off.

"Witnesses will state that this has not been opened since you last entered it, Doyle. . . . Come in, gentlemen."

Sleepy then began to tear up the flooring with a crowbar and shortly there were revealed cat-track pins, detonators and all manner of necessary small equipment.

"The cats were bait, Doyle," said Sleepy. "Bainsly here can tell you all about such things. You wanted to slow us down and you thought you did. You would have gotten an entire planet remake for nothing, and transportation for your colonists as well, if this sabotage had succeeded. But you didn't kill any men, and so I don't think my company will make a charge. You'll have to talk it over with Bainsly, of course, but unless you've got nine million cash here and now, Planetary Engineering Construction Co., Inc., will be putting up one planet for auction. And that's profitable enough, Doyle."

The inspection party had left early in the afternoon, taking the hope of Colonial Enterprises with them. Barteber was getting dinner and singing about a "gal who wouldn't say her prayers," and Tommer sat listening to the sad, sad fate of that creature.

Tommer's gaze shifted to the visograph and the stud poker game with Mart Lonegan.

Mart was winning today and his debt was down to eighteen thousand dollars.

"Mr. McGee," Tommer said at last, "do you think it would take me very long to learn stud poker?"

"Why no, Tommer. Not at all. In fact, I'd be willing to teach you myself."

The Obsolete Weapon

The Obsolete Weapon

RATS squeaked, vermin scuttled, drunks stank and the noisome dark oppressed. The American Military Prison in Rome was exceedingly unkind to the senses.

Now that the *Tedeschi* had fled northward, American arms sought to integrate a conquest and a people.

In the dankest, foulest cell that G-2 could provide, a brace of allegedly choice criminals kept diffident company.

"Anguis in herba!" howled one from the caldron of his troubled slumber. This, and the other Latin gibberish he had screamed, did not soothe his companion, who now finally protested.

Danny West was some minutes pulling himself from the muddy maelstrom of his nightmares, but at last he scrubbed his eyes with horny knuckles and blinked nervously at his companion.

"You were dreaming," said his cellmate.

"If that was a dream," said Danny West, "then this cell is Allah's number one Paradise!"

"You're an American, aren't you?" queried his cellmate with polite interest.

"Sure, from Teague County, Texas!"

"Then why the Latin?"

Danny West scuttled backward two feet and watched from there, gaping suspiciously.

"What Latin?" he said.

"You just called somebody 'a snake in the grass.'"

Danny hedged. "Well, he was . . . well . . . er— Forget it!"

"Don't get me wrong," said his cellmate. "You've got me curious, that's all. What are you, an American soldier, doing with a mouth full of Latin?"

"I was associate professor of ancient languages before they snatched me into this cockeyed mess," said Danny West. He was plainly hoping to change the subject. "Lay it to *aqua vitae*."

"Oh, I wouldn't say so. From what I could pick up—"

Danny West looked dangerous.

"Shut up!" he said. "Shut up! Leave me alone!"

There was quiet then, the cellmate having retired offendedly to the farthest corner, where he sat brooding for more than half an hour.

The feeling that he had given offense wore upon Danny. The screaming urge within him to communicate drove him further. At last he crossed the cell and sat down on the blanket alongside his cellmate.

"Have a cigarette," he said by way of apology.

The cellmate took one, looked at it for some time as though doubtful what one must do with such an article. At last he permitted it to be lighted, and drew on it carefully.

"I guess I'd better tell you," said Danny West, the flashboards tearing away from the top of his conversational dam. "I've got to tell somebody! Or I'll begin to think I'm crazy myself."

His cellmate put a lazy guard on his interest. "By all means," he said. "Fire away."

70

Well—said Danny West—about twenty-four hours ago I was fighting for my life harder than anybody at any training camp ever dreamed of. And the kind of fighting I was doing wasn't included in any training manuals either.

I haven't fought the Germans yet, but when it comes to that, after what I've been through I'll take my chances.

You know how it was yesterday afternoon, just about like it is now, the air hot and thick and a storm coming on. Our outfit had been coming forward for two days without any rest and all yesterday we walked in dust behind tanks for what seemed like fifteen million years.

I was tired. Everybody was tired. But when we got into the city it seemed everybody from the commanding general down had some lousy fatigue duty for us to do. There wasn't any outfit in the army except Company B of the Nineteenth.

Me, after I put about eighteen billets in shape for other guys to sleep in, I finally got routed out by that stinking captain of ours and told that I had been detailed to reinforce the local MP company. He said there were going to be a lot of riots and that two squads were to go and stand duty for any emergency that came up. We were flying squads.

It had been getting hotter and hotter. Some big clouds slid in over Rome, and finally opened up with enough artillery to end the war.

Our captain marched us down to the Colosseum and then left us standing there in the rain, while he went off to some soft bunk someplace.

The sergeant watched him go and the rest of us tried to

find a dry spot under the stones. Then the sergeant said, "I got to make a routine patrol," and he disappeared.

Then one of the corporals said, "I got to make a routine patrol, too," and *he* disappeared. And the first thing I knew there wasn't anybody left there but me.

Pretty soon this stinking captain of ours came back and in the course of that time I was sound asleep—rain, mud and all. He gave me a swift kick in the side and says, "On your feet! Attention! What do you mean by sleeping on duty? Where are the others?"

So I says, "They're out making routine patrols, Captain."

"I'll routine patrol them," he says and stamps off, probably to find some place a lot drier than it was outside the Colosseum.

I walked up and down for a few minutes but there wasn't anything doing. The population of Rome just wasn't thinking about rioting. It was either kissing the boots of the conquering army, or shacking up, or drowning its sorrows in *vino*.

They had given us riot guns, a couple of bandoliers of ammunition apiece, and three tear gas grenades per man. Then they took away our own weapons, the only ones we knew how to use, as being too heavy for street fighting.

The gun I was carrying must have been made for the Franco-Prussian War. I sat down and looked at it a little while and tried to figure out how the thing worked. I had nothing better to do and you never know in the middle of a war when you're going to need your weapons.

I had to make up my own manual about the thing as I went along, but later on I was sure glad that I'd taken the trouble. The old baby was an automatic shotgun weighing about fifteen pounds, with an eight-gauge barrel that would have fitted better on a howitzer. It was fully automatic and its ammunition would have broken the springs on a lorry.

I got tired when I was sure the captain wasn't coming back and began to look for a dry hole under the stones. The lightning kept cracking down like the end of the world. The rain had stopped falling in drops and had joined hands to make close formation. You had to have gills to breathe in that weather.

So I found this hole, and I crawled in. About two seconds later a lightning bolt hit the top of the Colosseum and showered enough mortar down to rebuild a village. That's all I know.

Immediately afterwards I was awakened by the roaring of wild beasts. It was as though a circus tent had caught on fire and the menagerie was fighting its way out. It was a symphony of racket that made the ground shake under me. From the bass roars of the lions to the yelps of the dogs, the voice of every animal could be picked out of that din. Cutting through it, weaving circles around it, slicing it up and tramping it down were the trumpetings of at least a hundred wild elephants.

I was lying in straw and the sun was bright through bars. The straw stank, the animals stank, and I was scared. Plainly, somebody had done me dirt.

The walls about me were of wood, except on one side where a grating barred my way. There was no exit that I could find, and my speculations ran the limit from military prison to a new war machine of the *Tedeschi*.

It was morning, but I had not slept. I was still soaked with the rain, which a moment before I knew had been falling.

I didn't really begin to shake, though, until a hideous crescendo of human screams began to shake the building. There was enough agony in those screams to load a freight train.

My explorations grew swift and I discovered presently that I was not in a cell but in a sort of hallway, one end of which was blocked by the iron grate, the other end by a large wooden door. On the other side of the latter I could hear a swelling, murmuring sound, like a crowd at a football game.

I still had my riot gun, three gas grenades, and, I hoped, my wits. I was about to shoot the lock off the wooden door when a small black dwarf came wriggling up to the iron bars and peered through. He looked, gaped, and quickly ran away.

I yelled for him to come back, and so he did, with a man whose dress had unmistakably not been seen on earth for the last two thousand years.

He was a big man. With one hand he carried a bucket full of live coals and in the other hand he had a long glowing poker. His face was brutal, like a gorilla's.

"Listen, fellows," I said, "how about letting me out of here?"

They stared at each other and began a long argument which was punctuated by jabs toward the little man by the big man's hot poker.

For two or three minutes I could make nothing of the conversation until it came to me that they were talking Latin.

I had taught eight straight semesters of Latin at Texas

A&M, so it did not take me long to enter into the spirit of the thing.

"Get me out of here," I demanded.

"He's no Christian," said the big man.

"Well, then he's a northman," said the dwarf.

"Northman or no northman, he's no gladiator. What are we supposed to do?"

"Get a gladiator and put him in," said the dwarf.

"All right, you run and get Glaucus, and ask him to come here." The big man turned toward me. "Who put you in here?"

"I'm Danny West from Teague County, Texas, and if I don't get out of here pretty quick and report to duty, my captain will make mincemeat out of me. Lemme out of here."

"What kind of a gladiator are you?" he demanded.

"I'm no gladiator, I'm a soldier. And if you don't listen to reason, the United States Army is going to be mighty peeved at me."

"You're a gladiator all right, you're just scared. A taste of this iron will cure that. But what are you supposed to fight?"

"Fight? I'm not mad at anybody."

"What d'ya fight? What d'ya fight with? Net and spear? Lions? What?" The big man waved his poker suggestively, and seeing that it had cooled during the argument, thrust it back into the glowing coals.

"I fight Germans," I said.

"Yes, yes, what Roman won't fight barbarians, but I mean in the arena. What d'ya fight in the arena?"

"The . . . the arena . . . ?"

A swelling roar hammered at the wooden door. And a flock of history lit in my lap like a stack of iron plates.

"Well, what d'ya fight?" he persisted.

"Mice," I said. We were getting nowhere.

"What kind of a weapon is that? You can't do anything against lions with a club. No, nor . . ." he scratched a leprous scalp at the problem.

A small, nervous individual, dripping sweat, came streaming up to the bars.

"Who is this? What is this? Oh, I'm ruined. I can never set up a good program unless some fool gums it up. Oh, why was I ever born? What made me ever get into this business? Arrangements, arrangements, arrangements . . . One minute it's 'Send the Christians in first.' The next minute it's 'Make it Nubians and lions.' By the guts of Jupiter, I'll retire. That's what I'll do, I'll retire."

"We didn't know he was in here," said the big man. "I left Jocko here."

"Bunglers! Fools! Idiots!" howled the dripping master of ceremonies. "The crowd is getting ugly. That last batch of Christians sat down in the middle of the arena and let the wild dogs run all over them, without lifting a hand. Oh, what poor fodder they send me these days! How can I put on a show—? Take him out of there. Take him out of there quick. The next act is about to go on. Get Glaucus. Oh, oh, oh, do something! *Do* something!"

But before they could do anything, there was a creak, and a groan, and then silence. The big wooden door had slid up and the white sand of the arena blinded me.

Behind me the master of ceremonies groaned piteously, "It's too late now—it's too late. Throw some lions at him and let's get it over with."

"Get out there, you," said the man with the poker, which he used to good effect. I jumped!

"Now see here," I said. But I had jumped so far that I stood outside the door and it dropped with a bang behind me.

I swear there must have been ten thousand people in the seats around the arena. The sun was beating down and the air was full of dust and yells. Boos and catcalls split through the lower, steadier roar of the crowd.

One section was stamping its feet and shouting in time. "Bring on the Nubians! We want the Nubians! Bring on the Nubians!" I felt a little bit insulted that they would prefer Nubians to me. But they didn't know me, after all.

There were pools of blood indifferently spread with white sand all around me. The once-white palisades which lifted fourteen feet from the ground to the first boxes were splattered with dried gore. The stench of the place was horrible. Death—rotten meat—and unwashed humanity. I had stage fright.

You couldn't have heard an artillery barrage in the din that rocked the old place. I was trying feebly to collect my wits and find a way out of all this. I had got well into the realization that something terrible indeed had happened to me, when the wooden gates at the far end from me opened—out bounded the biggest lion I ever laid my eyes on this side of the Galveston Zoo.

This lion had something on his mind. His eyes were so red they practically dripped blood. He was so thin that you could see light straight through the middle of him. His tail was ten feet long, or longer, and it was lashing from side to side until you could almost hear it swish. Apparently he was looking for something.

Shortly he found it. Me! I felt like saying, "Now wait a minute, fellows, let's sit down right where we are and think this whole thing over. I'm sure we can talk the matter into a reasonable solution."

But the crowd was in a hurry! And the lion was in a hurry! And the riot gun was strapped across my back. I had to do something and do it quick—so I did it!

I dropped on one knee, pried loose the gun, threw a shell under the hammer and took aim.

Now, shooting lions is not my favorite pastime. I had had a little experience with quail, and one small experience with a deer that got away, but not lions. And the front sight of that gun was weaving around like it was trying to write my obituary.

The lion got within ten feet, crouched down till his belly touched the sand, and then jumped!

There was a blast against my shoulder that knocked me about two feet! When I picked myself up the lion was lying there, all four feet reaching for clouds and clawing.

Though I had been told that hunters were usually pretty proud of their first kill, I never had time to examine this one. They let twelve more lions in through the second door.

The newcomers wasted no time. They saw the dying lion—saw me—and began to whet their appetites at ninety miles an hour. They crossed that arena, the whole twelve of them, like they'd just heard chow call.

The lion got within ten feet, crouched down till his belly touched the sand, and then jumped!

I looked to the blunderbuss. They had not even given us instructions as to how to fire the thing, for it was an English gun and they probably didn't know themselves. Like a shotgun it fired paper shells and I was afraid these had swollen in the rain. It fired a mass of pellets something bigger than buckshot and with a very wide spread. Though a few of them would discourage rioters, what did these lions know about the Riot Act?

I watched them sweep down on me. Did you ever see a lion run? Well, mister, they don't run at all, they bound sideways off the ground like rubber balls. A jeep on a Roman road would make a better target.

I put that old museum piece of a shotgun on single and set myself down to knock off the leaders before the main crowd arrived.

Their stink got there before they did. A lion smells like a combination of a slaughterhouse, a choice privy and a dead horse in August. The odor of it, added to my stage fright, was enough to make me lose my boots.

The old gun belted me in the shoulder. The leader plowed sand for fifteen feet. The top of his head was gone! Clean as if he'd patronized an army barbershop.

The face of the next one just plain disappeared.

The third did five forward somersaults and ended up with his tail pointing at me accusatively. Then came the main herd.

I slipped the gun to full automatic and let them have it! There were only eleven shells to go, but they sure were plenty. There was lion meat stacked around there, until it looked as though I had decided to build a castle of the stuff.

I remembered how they'd used to feed poor old horses to the lions at the Galveston Zoo. I felt pretty satisfied, let me tell you.

I had a breather then. I wiped the smoke out of my eyes and looked around me. I sure thought I'd shown the locals a thing or two. A whiff of the crowd hit me and it stunk almost as bad as the lions. The masses of streamers and faces went up from me on all sides like ranges of mountains. The crowd was quiet and I fully expected them to be something more than curious. However, it evidently took a great deal to shake a Roman mob.

I looked at one side where the President of the Games, the Emperor, for all I knew, and two royal ladies gazed on with indifferent contempt.

They were wearing gold laurel leaves inset with jewels. The box looked like Christmas. On their right sat what I took to be the vestal virgins, white-hooded and grim. Most of them, startlingly enough, were quite old. Above me, out of the quiet, drifted the voice of a young buck talking to his girl.

"Like Nero, isn't it, to produce magic in the arena. No taste, I've always said, no taste whatever. This fellow is simply one of those wizards from Assyria that we've heard about lately. Mass hypnotism, you know. There were no lions at all. We merely suppose that they are dead. The thing is really quite simple."

"Gee, Marius," said the girl, "you know everything, don't you?"

The one section of the stands which had been chanting before had now recovered from its surprise and began to demand blood. "We want Numidians. We want Numidians.

We want Numidians," they chanted, stamping their feet in time.

"Now take earlier this morning," said young Marius, in a bored tone, "those elephants squashing the Christians, now there's what I call a spectacle. And that one elephant that picked up the woman and knocked her head off against the wall. Now that was interesting. But this sort of thing, mere wizardry, chicanery . . ."

The crowd went back to buying nuts and fruit off the vendors. Some other parts of the crowd began to take up the Numidian chant.

I was trying hard to recall how these games were conducted. I finally remembered that after one had killed his meat or his man, he was supposed to go before the President's box and ask for the thumbs up or thumbs down sign. So, I began walking toward the President's box.

I was getting my breath back by now, for it seemed to me that the worst was over. The crowd was becoming quite impatient with the delay and, as the master of ceremonies had said, was obviously in an ugly mood. Boos, hisses, catcalls and an occasional hunk of rotten fruit began to descend into the arena.

"We want action," bawled a tubby man above the palisades. "We came here to see a spectacle. We want action. We want blood!"

Others in the crowd began to take up his chant. Soon the ground under my feet was shivering with it. I never did get close to the President's box. For, about halfway en route, the tone of the crowd changed so quickly and to such a pitch of enthusiasm that I knew I was in for more.

The master of ceremonies was evidently on his toes. I turned around quickly. A gate was opening and two net-and-trident men sped out into the arena, holding up their weapons for acclaim. They were evidently quite popular, for they were greeted with cheering.

They wasted little time, for a fast victory was what was wanted. They closed in. One circled wide until he had gained a distance on my left. The other held his ground on my right. Then they rushed me!

I didn't like to do what I did. But I dropped to one knee and leveled on the first one.

BOWIE!

He flew apart in mid-rush.

I swiveled around and found the other one within ten feet of me. Startled by the fate of his friend, he drew and then pitched his trident at me. Its middle prong hit my helmet with a clang, and the weapon went zooming off in a new direction.

He spread and cast the net before I could catch him in my sights. The thing settled over me like a thousand spider webs.

He rushed to retrieve his trident and had picked it up when—

BOWIE!

He went to join his companion on the banks of the Styx.

"Boo!" yelled the crowd. "Boo! Magic! Fake!"

Nevertheless, I approached the President's box again. I stood beneath it. If this was Nero, then I had not looked to find the handsome young fellow that he was. A dissolute mouth was all that marred his face. I took the woman on his right to be his mother and sweetheart, Agrippina.

He rushed to retrieve his trident and
had picked it up when—

"Boo! Fake!" screamed the crowd.

Nero looked over the edge of his box at me. Ceremoniously he raised his right hand. And then, with a savage gesture, struck his thumb down.

This appeared very silly to me since there was no other combatant in the arena, and I certainly was not flat on my back awaiting a coup.

The crowd echoed the sentiment and the master of ceremonies must have been looking, for within the space of a minute, three doors opened and at least seventy-five Numidians dashed with a war cry into the arena.

Each one of them looked about fifteen feet tall, shiny black, wearing ostrich plumes and carrying assegais. They danced, and bounded, and waved their weapons and leather shields. They drew up into a formation approaching a phalanx and, after pausing long enough to be acclaimed, started for me.

I turned sideways and yelled at Nero, "Hey, you, this isn't fair!" Nero grinned ghoulishly at me. I turned back and looked at the Numidians.

I was scared. My blood clogged my veins. Maybe it was the war cry, maybe it was the shiny black bodies, maybe it was the savage teeth. But the one place where I wanted to be at that minute was back in Teague County, Texas, eating some of my mother's corn bread.

I had reloaded the riot gun in front of the President's box, but I knew better than to try to spray that mob.

Something was banging against my hip. I recalled the tear gas grenades. I unhooked one and pulled its pin. I counted to three and chucked it. It burst immediately before the phalanx and sprayed dots of white smoke in all directions. The Numidians vanished in a cloud of it.

All of a sudden I felt like laughing. Maybe it was hysteria, but those black boys had looked so gay and so brave dancing in, that the contrast was very funny. They came out of that cloud in the formation of scattered rabbits. They were doubling up, and wailing, and clawing at their eyes. They were calling out the names of their various gods and rolling on the ground.

Their shields and spears were thrown in all directions. However, the crowd was not amused.

"Boo! Fake!" they jeered.

But the Numidians didn't jeer. They went over to the edge and found places to sit down, or they bumped into each other, or they tried to climb up the palisades. It came to me that they were more scared than hurt.

"Charge me, will you?" I yelled at 'em. Then I went out to pick me up a cluster of ostrich plumes, hoping that this act would mollify the crowd.

During this operation it seemed to me suddenly that I was acting very foolishly. Here I had all the weapons that they didn't have, obsolete as I considered them, and all I needed to do was to blast the lock on one of those doors and walk out of the place.

There was little enjoyment in the arena for me. Sooner or later somebody was going to get hurt.

I threw down the ostrich plumes and rushed toward one of the doors. But there the Roman guards threw the dice for me and got "crap."

That door came open with a bang! And there I was, looking

down the trunk of the biggest Indian elephant that was ever born. If P. T. Barnum had seen that elephant, he would have gone crazy and billed him all over the world. That elephant was so huge he could have used the Empire State Building for a toothpick. What made him look all the more horrible, they had thrust burning sticks and barbs under his skin until he looked like a porcupine.

Somebody—probably my old friend—was jabbing him with a red hot poker from behind. And the elephant came out of there!

He saw me!

He was delighted!

He reared up until there was an eclipse of the sun. He aimed two feet twice as big as kettledrums right at my head.

His tusks gleamed. His teeth gleamed. His eyes gleamed. And froth sprayed out of his mouth like a flame-thrower.

Hurrahs and hurrays bounded around that arena from a delighted crowd.

I had brought up so short at the sight of this world-ender that I sat down, directly under him. The butt of the riot gun hit alongside of me. My finger threw it on full automatic and I let him have the entire chamber as fast as I could shoot.

Pieces of elephant meat flew all over the arena, the palisades and me. When he hit earth again his trunk slammed me sideways about thirty feet. I picked myself up. But there was no more fight left in that elephant.

These people were getting too rough to suit my fancy and once more I started to get out of there. A scream of surprise and delight from the crowd made me turn again.

He saw me!
He was delighted!
He reared up until there was an eclipse of the sun. . . .
His tusks gleamed. His teeth gleamed. His eyes gleamed.

A second elephant, twice as big as the first one, had been let into the arena! He was bearing down on me like a combination of the Graf Zeppelin and a General Sherman tank. My error was that I was the only one in motion in that arena. He ran over about five Numidians getting to me.

The Society for the Prevention of Cruelty to Animals will probably never hear about this, but my riot gun was empty. There was nothing else I could do.

I unhooked a second gas grenade from my belt and pulled the pin. When he was within thirty feet of me I heaved it into his open mouth.

BOWIE!

That elephant's head like to have torn off. He couldn't stop because he was going too fast. His front legs folded up and his hind end came on over them. I jumped sideways just in time to miss him. He did two complete somersaults and wound up with a crash against the boards right underneath Nero's box.

I was surprised, to say the least. I hadn't expected a tear gas bomb to kill him. But from the look of the way he was heaving and shuddering, that elephant was halfway to his happy hunting ground already.

The little torches jammed into his side began to flicker out. The smoke from them drifted around him like a shroud.

The Numidians had drawn off to the farthest point of the arena. The crowd now took to jeering at them. Two of them advanced as though to prove their metal. The riot gun took care of that.

"Let me out of here," I yelled at Nero. "I'm Danny West of Teague County, Texas. And you'd better be careful next time where you get your gladiators. Let me out of here!"

But Nero Germanicus and his party were not thinking about gladiators. The tear gas had fumed out through the twitching trunk of the elephant. It had wheezed from his scalded lungs to work its way upward and drift into the President's box. His mother and the ladies of the court had scrambled awkwardly backwards to the walkway above. Nero now stood crying the first and last tears of his merciless life.

I glanced around the arena. The crowd was plainly scared. And that, my friend, is an accomplishment, for the impressing of a Roman crowd was a thing for which men sold their lives. It began to come over me what I had done.

I looked around me. That arena looked like a dance hall after the Longshoremen's Ball. Dead lions and elephants were stacked up like the Chicago stockyards. Numidians, dead, wounded or terrified, were black or red spots on the white sand. Above them the crowd was beginning to surge away from the palisades.

I could see young Marius and his girl. From the expression on his face, he had ceased to be convinced of the authenticity of necromancy.

I swelled out my chest and strutted a little bit. Such was my confidence that I missed a second vital fact—when a Roman crowd gets scared, it kills.

And when a Caesar is offended . . .

Up until this time I had not paid particular attention to the

glittering helmets and shining spears of the household troops
which surrounded the box of Nero Germanicus Caesar. They
were fine, big Germans. And, though they might have been
the ancestors of the *Tedeschi* we were supposed to fight in
Italy, they were very far from bones. Six feet six, most of them,
picked for their size and courage. They served Caesar with
a fanaticism born of the fact that without Caesar alive they
themselves were dead before the Roman mob. So little was
Nero Germanicus loved at this time, that he was accustomed
to placing large troops about the city.

So it happened, on this luckless day, that the Tenth Legion
with all its panoply and fine training from across the Rhine
was home and at hand.

I saw the courier go, and though I didn't know his message,
I decided not to stay. The stiffening legs of the elephant and
his massive body made a sort of a ladder up to the box. Of
this I took advantage.

I know more about mounting horses than elephants, but
this one was bottom side up. I scrambled to his belly and
then up his leg to grab at the top of the palisade. I was very
engrossed in my effort since my equipment was not light and
I was carrying that riot gun handy, reloaded. It was only a
cheer from the crowd which made me look up.

I was staring at the points of twenty leveled spears, backed
by the blond beards of the household guard.

Behind them and above them Caesar was smiling. It was
his trick. I heaved myself down off that leg and under the
protection of the elephant while all twenty of those spears

bit meat close behind me. But it was elephant meat, not Texan.

I stuck my head up again through the small forest and I leveled the riot gun. Three of the bodyguards had already begun to come down the elephant's leg. They came down all right.

BOWIE! BOWIE! BOWIE!

Tedeschi! Well, I'd come to Italy to fight Germans, but I didn't know that I would find them in the accoutrements of Roman Legionnaires. The riot gun let out a long roar. And the palisade above me was cleared! I reloaded and again stormed the ramparts.

I don't know where they came from, but they sure came in a hurry. Plumes, spears and helmets jammed the runway which led outward from the President's box. The Tenth Legion was on its way.

The Roman mob was cheering itself into laryngitis. All of a sudden I got mad.

They'd come to see blood. Well, they were going to get blood. That riot gun blew down the first ranks of the Tenth Legion like a lawnmower. Their armor corselets might as well have been made of papier-mâché. The Numidians had been whipped up till now, but they knew that they would die anyway unless they did something. So I received a rear attack.

Other companies of the Tenth Legion were flooding down into the arena from the boxes on either side of the President's box. It was getting hot. I realized that it was certainly no place for Danny West.

I pulled the pin on the last tear gas bomb and pitched it up into the runway behind the President's box where it jetted white.

I dodged about twenty spears and got up on the elephant again. From there I gave 'em a full burst from the riot gun. I reached the palisade and climbed over into the chair that Nero had so recently occupied.

If the simple act of grabbing a throne would have made me Caesar, then I was Caesar. But I was sure sorry for it. You've seen it rain in a hurricane down in Galveston? Well, those big, long slanting drops weren't anything compared to the number of javelins that were in the air around me then.

One clanged off my helmet and almost knocked me silly. Some archer got to work and began to stud the woodwork with arrows. Ahead of me I could see the open runway, cleared now.

I shut my eyes to dash through the tear gas. Then came the main bulk of the Tenth Legion. They blocked that exit like pickets make a fence. I backed up. I turned to see that the crowd itself, with cushions and baskets for weapons, had begun to back up the remaining Legionnaires, household troops and Numidians. All it required now was a pack of wild dogs and another flock of lions to make this a real Roman holiday.

I let the riot gun go back into that press and then grabbed for the bandolier to reload. There was just one chamberful left. People were behind me and above me, Legionnaires were in front of me and, in short, it was no place for a self-respecting Texan boy to be found.

Right about then I figured I was just so much lion meat. But I started up the ramp intending to find another way out. Then the impossible happened.

I fell flat on my face, slipping in the blood which spattered the runway. And before I could regain my feet a bolt of lightning hit the Colosseum.

It missed Nero, who had probably fled to the Palatine Hill by then. But it sure made hash out of the rest of the crowd.

I hid my face in my arms but it didn't come near me. It was a funny kind of lightning. It rolled around the arena in big yellow flashes. The whole crowd either dived under seats or died where they stood.

The Tenth Legion, versed in all the lore of ancient superstition, saw that lightning and left their spears behind them.

I scrambled to my feet, but I got up a split second too soon. There was somebody above me. And he was yelling. I couldn't make out anything in the roar of that arena. This guy came over the side of the runway and lit beside me. But Danny West wasn't waiting to be detained.

I let him have a clip alongside of the neck and grabbed at his hands which I figured held a knife. Something came away and then I fell. About ten million volts of lightning went around the place once again.

That's all I know until I woke up being kicked in the side. It was raining. It was morning. It was Rome. And from the empty sardine can alongside of me I knew that the army of occupation was at hand.

"Get out of that, you deserter!" said this stinking captain of ours.

I looked up and I swear I could almost have kissed the guy, as much as I hated him.

"Where have you been?" he demanded. "What have you been doing? What do you mean by dishonoring me and disgracing your company?" And then, without waiting for me to answer any of these questions, he launched into a tirade that would have done credit to a West Pointer.

He told me that I was guilty, as near as I could gather, of at least twenty-nine of the first thirty articles of war. Not the least of which was pusillanimous conduct in the face of the enemy.

It seems there had been a riot the night before and I hadn't been there. Though I tried to convince that stinking captain that I had been in a riot that made *his* look mighty pale, there wasn't any talking past that high-grade flow of official redundancy.

He had two MPs onto me like setter pups after a quail. He took the riot gun away from me and booted me all the way down to the military prison. So here I am, and all I got to show for it is this here fountain pen I took out of that bird's hand just before the lights went out.

He held up a small gray object to his cellmate and relapsed, looking glum.

His cellmate looked at him pensively.

"Well?" demanded Danny West pugnaciously. "Go ahead and call me a liar."

His cellmate regarded the souvenir critically.

"And where did you have it?" he said.

Danny West gestured at his boot: "In here. Them damned MPs would take your gold teeth off of you."

The cellmate seemed a bit nervous.

"Let me see it."

"Okay, but you've got to hand it right back."

Danny West extended it to him, nearly dropping it. His cellmate turned white and grabbed it just before it touched pavement. Caressingly he looked it over, wrapped it in his handkerchief and thrust it in his pocket. He stood up.

"See here," protested Danny West, "where you going with that?"

"It happens, regrettably, that it belongs to me," said his cellmate.

"You? Now look here, I took that off a guy . . ." A dawning expression came over Danny West. He jumped to his feet and pointed. "Then you—"

"Yes," said the cellmate, bowing slightly.

"But how . . . ?"

His cellmate deepened the bow and took from his pocket a small metal card not much bigger than a dog tag, but made of some glittering substance of which Danny West had no acquaintance. The Texan read it with growing awe.

"We didn't intend to land here," said the cellmate, "but we were caught without water and, unfortunately, the navigator and the captain chose the middle of the Italian desert in which to find it. We have not been much acquainted with these things for some time so you will excuse our ignorance.

"I used a certain device of ours to go back to a period when water had been there. But, unfortunately, I got somewhat scrambled in my dates. And your little show in the arena—which, by the way, I wouldn't have missed for worlds—sidetracked me further into this place."

He was moving toward the door as though his mere gesture would open it.

"But here," he said, "I won't be too hard on you. I'm sure if you tell the captain that your part in the riots was well played, proving it by your empty bandoliers, he will be very happy to let you off—particularly since you can make him a present of one of the jewels in these."

Saying which, he drew out of his knapsack the gold laurel wreaths which had been worn by Nero Germanicus and his consorts. He handed them to Danny West. And even in that gloom, the roundcut gems gleamed. The gold was so soft you could bend it with a finger.

"You won them fairly," said the cellmate. "Anybody but Nero would have considered the show quite good enough, without turning loose the Tenth Legion on you."

Danny West was agape. "But look here, how . . . ?"

"It's simply that I got to Rome when I should have gone to Carthage," said his cellmate. "Now, if you'll give me my identification."

Danny West read it again. The rest of his life those words would be engraved on his memory:

MORTAN, DAGGER B. 116335
MECHANIC FIRST CLASS, ROCKET TURBINES
INTER-SYSTEM SPACEWAYS
INOCULATED 10 JOLY 2595
BLOOD TYPE O

Danny West gave it up, numb with awe. His cellmate was applying a small gadget to the lock which dripped in large globules of iron upon the pavement.

"But wait a minute," said Danny West, "that lightning . . . That must have been . . ."

"Yes," said his cellmate, "this little gadget which you so carelessly supposed to be a fountain pen was the author of that. It's not very much. The pile cell in it is almost worn out. It's a sort of obsolete weapon, you see."

His cellmate walked through the swinging door, and then seemingly through the solid rock wall.

A long time after he had gone, Danny West stood, arms hanging limply, still holding the laurel wreaths, his mouth forming the parting words:

"An obsolete weapon!"

Story Preview

Story Preview

NOW that you've just ventured through some of the captivating tales in the Stories from the Golden Age collection by L. Ron Hubbard, turn the page and enjoy a preview of *Greed*. Join George Marquis Lorrilard, sometime lieutenant in the United Continents Space Navy—that pitiful handful of space guards—and now a space exploiter. Far in the future exist two Earth empires, separated by a weapon-projected wall of space and poised for war. Supposedly driven by greed, Lorrilard must change the fate of Earth and the stars.

Greed

IT can be said with more than a little truth that a society is lost when it loses its greed, for without hunger as a whip—for power, money or fame—man sinks into a blind sloth and, contented or not, is gone.

There were three distinct classes of men who made up the early vanguard into space—and they were all greedy.

First were the explorers, the keen-eyed, eager and dauntless few who wrenched knowledge from the dark and unwilling depths of the universe.

Next were the rangers, called variously the "space tramps," "space nuts" and "star hobos," who wandered aimlessly, looking, prospecting, seeing what was to be seen and wandering on.

And last were the exploiters, the hardheaded, quick-eyed and dangerous few who accomplished, according to a standard and learned work of the times, the "rape of space."

Each had his hunger. The explorer wanted knowledge and fame and he often laid down his life in an effort to attain them. The space tramp wanted novelty, change, adventure and sojourns in the exotic humanoid societies or solitudes in the wastes. The exploiter wanted gems and gold.

Hard words have been used against these last and it has been charged that their depredations in the first days of conquest committed ravages upon new planets which hundreds of generations could not repair.

George Marquis Lorrilard, sometime lieutenant in the United Continents Space Navy—that pitiful handful of space guards—was an exploiter. The savage libels leveled at him in his days are leveled even now. In the kindest histories, he is "not quite nice." And yet this man broke an impasse of Earth nations which threatened the future of all space conquest and planted the first successful colony in the stars.

He wanted wealth and he made no secret of it. A lean, hardy, ice-eyed man, Lorrilard knew his own desires and he attained them. Lesser men were afraid of him and yet, when one reviews the evidence, he never gave his own kind reason.

Often savage, always decisive and abrupt, George Marquis Lorrilard looms like a giant among his kind. He attained his goals. His fortune, wrested from brutal and inhospitable worlds, at one time amounted to twice the entire national debt of the United Continents and when it was at last dispersed in the reading of his will, it nearly wrecked Earth's economy.

But if one seeks to envision him as a palm-rubbing skinflint, cowering behind underlings, one is wrong. Even if that is the impression vengeful historians seek to give, nothing could be further from truth. He commanded his own ships. He fought his own fights. And he died in the act of personal conquest in the stars.

Not too long after exploration had begun in earnest, men found that there was wealth to be had amongst the alien worlds. All they saw, then, was the portable wealth, the fabulous jewels and precious metals and elements, which lay either already mined in the hands of hapless humanoids or was to be had by the merest skimming of the virgin ground. Some of the tales told in these times are not exaggerations. It is actually true that there was an entire mountain of solid gold on Durak and that there was a ruby measuring eighty feet in diameter on Psycho. The humanoids of Darwin of Mizar used solid silver for paving. And into a thousand worlds went the exploiters, close behind the explorers, to extract their due with pick and gun. They fought animals, humanoids, men and absolute zero—some died and some received their pay.

Few had thought of colonies at this time. Overpopulation on Earth was serious, but the first efforts with Mars had proven so pale that thoughts of new human worlds were few. Earth, as always, was too engrossed in her own travails to think much, as an entire society, about the stars.

An invention had disrupted affairs entirely. And it was a sudden and stopping thing. Heretofore, nearly all research had aided space conquest but now, abruptly, the problems of the Universe had to wait. The Asian government had triumphed.

For many a long year there had been a single Earth, all properly patrolled and controlled by a single government. And the researches had become private affairs. Long sleep had lulled the salons, and the armor of their army and navy was almost sunk to rust. In the last year before the political cataclysm, the total United Nations appropriation for defense was less than one-tenth its expenditure for education, a thing which, while pretty, is not practical. And for a long, long while, the Asiatic races had slept.

Earth had, as we all know, several human races. But her most energetic were the Oriental and the Occidental. And the Occidental ruled and the Oriental endured. A country which had been called Russia had almost triumphed once. And then it had failed. Although ostensibly white, it was actually Oriental. Sunk into what it considered a trying servitude to the Occidental races, Asia struggled behind her hands and at length, with the One-Earth government grown feeble, struck with suddenness.

The wounds of a forgotten war had festered into a new invention. It was privately done. And it outstripped all the means of offense which could be employed against it.

It was a simple contrivance. We would call it very elementary now. But to Earth it came as a stunning reversal of affairs. It was a "cohesion projector." By using the force which keeps electrons and atoms together, rather than the force which blows them apart, space itself could be made into a solid wall. In an instant then, from a single generator, a column several hundred feet in diameter could be projected upwards for several thousand miles. It was not an elementary force screen such as those in early use to repel missile rockets. It was a solid, if invisible, wall. With a slightly greater frequency, it could have made matter, but they did not know that then and, indeed, did not find it out for another five hundred years.

With cunning handicraft, the Asian races, under the direction of the ex-federation of Russia, constructed their thousands of generators, passed them secretly to proper points for installation and suddenly announced, with the murder of all the United Nations garrisons within the boundaries of Asia, that they were free from the remainder of the world.

A dozen violent attacks against the rebels ended in defeat for the United Nations. The remaining political entities outside this barrier formed the United Continents under the direction of a major country in North America.

At first no one supposed that any great harm would come of this. The Asians knew better than to attack such excellent missile weapons as the United Continents had, and the United Continents had learned with cost not to attack the cohesion barriers of the Asians. Earth was in a fine state of deadlock and consequent intrigue, and stayed that way for many years.

It was into this strange situation that George Marquis Lorrilard was born. He went to the United Continents Naval Academy, was graduated in the center of his class, was given a minor warship assignment and was forgotten about as a cog in the machinery of government. In due time, unnoticed in general but always admired by his divisions for his athletic skill and competence, he became a lieutenant and was placed in command of an outer-space patrol vessel, the *State Sahara*.

Only then did he astonish anyone.

To find out more about *Greed* and how you can obtain your copy, go to www.goldenagestories.com.

Glossary

Glossary

STORIES FROM THE GOLDEN AGE *reflect the words and expressions used in the 1930s and 1940s, adding unique flavor and authenticity to the tales. While a character's speech may often reflect regional origins, it also can convey attitudes common in the day. So that readers can better grasp such cultural and historical terms, uncommon words or expressions of the era, the following glossary has been provided.*

---

alihipidile: made-up name for an animal.

Alpha Centauri: the triple-star system that is closest to the Earth.

anguis in herba: (Latin) a snake in the grass; a treacherous or harmful thing that is hidden or seemingly harmless.

aqua vitae: (Latin) literally "water of life"; used in current English to mean a strong distilled alcohol, especially a strong liquor such as whiskey or brandy.

assegais: slender iron-tipped hardwood spears used chiefly by African peoples.

Assyria: an ancient empire and civilization of western Asia, at its height between the ninth and seventh centuries BC.

The empire extended from the Mediterranean Sea across the Middle East.

auto-blinded: to have made oneself unable to notice or understand something.

bandolier: a broad belt worn over the shoulder by soldiers and having a number of small loops or pockets for holding cartridges.

banshees: (Irish legend) female spirits whose wailing warns of a death in a house.

beaters: people who drive animals out from cover.

bellowing: expanding to draw air in and compressing to force the air out.

billets: lodgings for soldiers.

blunderbuss: a short musket (gun) with expanded muzzle to scatter shot, bullets or slugs at close range.

boon: something to be thankful for; blessing; benefit.

Carthage: an ancient city in northern Africa.

cat: Caterpillar bulldozer; a heavy engineering vehicle used to push large quantities of soil, sand, rubble, etc., during construction work. It is made by Caterpillar, Inc., commonly referred to simply as *cat*.

cat men: operators of Caterpillar bulldozers.

Colosseum: an ancient amphitheatre in Rome.

corselets: body armor, especially breastplates.

coup: *coup de grâce*; a finishing stroke.

crap: a losing throw in the game of craps, where players wager money against the outcome of one roll, or a series of rolls, of two dice.

dark star: a theoretical star whose gravity is strong enough to trap light; mostly superseded by the concept of "black hole."

dint of, by: by vigorous and persistent means.

docks: any of various weedy plants that have broad leaves and clusters of small greenish or reddish flowers.

done me dirt: treated me unfairly or reprehensibly.

faring forth: traveling away from a particular place.

figger: figure.

flashboards: boards fitted at the top of a dam to add to its height and increase the amount of water that can be held back.

flying squads: trained, mobile groups of police officers capable of moving quickly into action and performing specialized tasks, as during an emergency.

Franco-Prussian War: (1870–1871) the war between France and Prussia. The conflict was a culmination of years of tension between the two powers, which finally came to a head over the issue of a candidate for the vacant Spanish throne following the deposition of the Queen of Spain. The French had equipped their infantry with the Chassepot, a breech-loading rifle with a maximum effective range of some 750 yards and a rapid reload time. Made famous as the arm of the French forces in this war, the Chassepots were responsible for most of the Prussian and other German casualties during the conflict.

G: gravity; a unit of acceleration equal to the acceleration of gravity at the Earth's surface.

G-2: United States Army Intelligence (a branch of the Army).

garnishee: to take the money or property of a debtor by legal authority.

G-men: government men; agents of the Federal Bureau of Investigation.

goon: a professional gangster whose work is beating up or terrorizing people.

Graf Zeppelin: a large dirigible named after the German pioneer of airships, Ferdinand von Zeppelin. It flew for the first time on September 18, 1928 and was the largest airship at that time at 776 feet (262.5 meters) in length.

Here's how: used as a toast.

hole card: the card dealt face down in the first round of a deal in stud poker.

howitzer: a cannon that has a comparatively short barrel, used especially for firing shells at a high angle of elevation for a short range, as for reaching a target behind cover or in a trench.

Lady Luck: luck or good fortune represented as a woman.

leaded ports: portholes with glass impregnated with a small amount of lead to impede radiation.

link pin: a thin rod that fastens together separate sections of a tread.

magnetrons: devices that generate high-frequency electromagnetic waves, as for use in radar applications.

make mincemeat out of: thrash, beat decisively.

Mercator: a type of high-quality world map shown on a flat surface that can be used for accurate navigation.

metal: mettle; spirited determination.

mitts: hands.

mix words: variant of "mince words"; to restrain oneself in a conversation and say less than one wants to, out of fear of offending the listener.

MP: Military Police.

net-and-trident: a pair of weapons used by gladiators consisting of a net and a three-pronged spear.

Nubians: people from Nubia, a region in southern Egypt and northern Sudan and a former kingdom from 2000 BC–AD 1400.

Numidians: people from Numidia, an ancient country in North Africa corresponding roughly to modern Algeria.

onion: one's subject or business.

out at elbows: in financial straits; short of funds.

Palatine Hill: one of seven hills in Rome; the central hill of the seven on which Rome was built, considered the oldest and the site of many of the imperial palaces.

palisades: stakes pointed at the top and set firmly in the ground in a close row with others to form a defense.

phalanx: especially in ancient Greece, a group of soldiers that attacks in close formation, protected by their overlapping shields and projecting spears.

privy: an outhouse.

P. T. Barnum: Phineas Taylor Barnum (1810–1891); an American showman who is best remembered for founding the circus that eventually became Ringling Brothers and Barnum and Bailey Circus.

radized: having caused (metal) to absorb doses of radiation.

Riot Act: an English statute of 1715 providing that if twelve or more persons assemble unlawfully and riotously, to the disturbance of the public peace, and refuse to disperse upon proclamation, they shall be considered guilty of a felony.

Roman holiday: a violent public spectacle or disturbance in which shame, degradation or physical harm is intentionally inflicted on one person or group by another or others. It comes from the bloody gladiatorial contests staged as entertainment for the ancient Romans.

Roman Legionnaires: members of the Roman army that was the basic military unit of ancient Rome. The Roman Legionnaires were the best equipped soldiers in the world, with helmets and armor that covered more than seventy percent of their bodies. They also carried a heavy body shield, two types of swords and a spear. They were well protected and their equipment was heavy, but still possessing considerable freedom of movement and lighter than the rest of the armies at the time.

scareheads: headlines in exceptionally large type.

Scheherazade: the female narrator of *The Arabian Nights,* who during one thousand and one adventurous nights saved her life by entertaining her husband, the king, with stories.

septuagenarian: a person who is seventy years of age.

shacking up: living or dwelling (in homes).

shooter: a person who sets off explosives in oil-drilling operations.

skinflint: one who is very reluctant to spend money; a miser.

skunked: cheated by someone.

spiderwork steel: steel; long rods of steel used for constructing antenna towers.

stiffen your resolution: to strengthen or make firm one's determination to do something or to carry out a purpose.

straw boss: a worker who also supervises a small work crew, acting as an assistant to the foreman.

stud poker: a game of poker in which the first round of cards is dealt face down, and the others face up.

Styx: (Greek mythology) river of Hades; the river across which the souls of the dead were ferried into the underworld.

Tedeschi: (Italian) Germans.

Tenth Legion: one of the legions used by Julius Caesar in 58 BC for his invasion of Gaul, an ancient European region.

Texas A&M: Texas Agricultural and Mechanical University located in College Station, Texas.

Treasury Department: an executive department of the US federal government that administers the treasury of the US government. The Internal Revenue Service (IRS) is the largest of the Treasury's bureaus. It is responsible for determining, assessing and collecting internal revenue in the US.

vestal virgins: (Roman mythology) virgin priestesses who tended the sacred fire in the temple of Vesta, goddess of the hearth.

visograph: a tool utilized for displaying still or moving images.

vitriol: sulfuric acid, a highly corrosive, dense, oily liquid.

West Pointer: someone from the US Military Academy, called West Point, in New York. It has been a military post since 1778 and the seat of the US Military Academy since 1802.

white: a white-colored chip having the lowest value, chiefly used in poker.

your queen bets: in stud poker, statement made by the dealer indicating who bets first. In this form of poker, the player with the highest card dealt in that round bets first.

L. Ron Hubbard
in the Golden Age
of Pulp Fiction

*In writing an adventure story
a writer has to know that he is adventuring
for a lot of people who cannot.
The writer has to take them here and there
about the globe and show them
excitement and love and realism.
As long as that writer is living the part of an
adventurer when he is hammering
the keys, he is succeeding with his story.*

*Adventuring is a state of mind.
If you adventure through life, you have a
good chance to be a success on paper.*

*Adventure doesn't mean globe-trotting,
exactly, and it doesn't mean great deeds.
Adventuring is like art.
You have to live it to make it real.*

—*L. RON HUBBARD*

L. Ron Hubbard
and American
Pulp Fiction

B ORN March 13, 1911, L. Ron Hubbard lived a life at least as expansive as the stories with which he enthralled a hundred million readers through a fifty-year career.

Originally hailing from Tilden, Nebraska, he spent his formative years in a classically rugged Montana, replete with the cowpunchers, lawmen and desperadoes who would later people his Wild West adventures. And lest anyone imagine those adventures were drawn from vicarious experience, he was not only breaking broncs at a tender age, he was also among the few whites ever admitted into Blackfoot society as a bona fide blood brother. While if only to round out an otherwise rough and tumble youth, his mother was that rarity of her time—a thoroughly educated woman—who introduced her son to the classics of Occidental literature even before his seventh birthday.

But as any dedicated L. Ron Hubbard reader will attest, his world extended far beyond Montana. In point of fact, and as the son of a United States naval officer, by the age of eighteen he had traveled over a quarter of a million miles. Included therein were three Pacific crossings to a then still mysterious Asia, where he ran with the likes of Her British Majesty's agent-in-place

L. Ron Hubbard, left, at Congressional Airport, Washington, DC, 1931, with members of George Washington University flying club.

for North China, and the last in the line of Royal Magicians from the court of Kublai Khan. For the record, L. Ron Hubbard was also among the first Westerners to gain admittance to forbidden Tibetan monasteries below Manchuria, and his photographs of China's Great Wall long graced American geography texts.

Upon his return to the United States and a hasty completion of his interrupted high school education, the young Ron Hubbard entered George Washington University. There, as fans of his aerial adventures may have heard, he earned his wings as a pioneering barnstormer at the dawn of American aviation. He also earned a place in free-flight record books for the longest sustained flight above Chicago. Moreover, as a roving reporter for *Sportsman Pilot* (featuring his first professionally penned articles), he further helped inspire a generation of pilots who would take America to world airpower.

Immediately beyond his sophomore year, Ron embarked on the first of his famed ethnological expeditions, initially to then untrammeled Caribbean shores (descriptions of which would later fill a whole series of West Indies mystery-thrillers). That the Puerto Rican interior would also figure into the future of Ron Hubbard stories was likewise no accident. For in addition to cultural studies of the island, a 1932–33

LRH expedition is rightly remembered as conducting the first complete mineralogical survey of a Puerto Rico under United States jurisdiction.

There was many another adventure along this vein: As a lifetime member of the famed Explorers Club, L. Ron Hubbard charted North Pacific waters with the first shipboard radio direction finder, and so pioneered a long-range navigation system universally employed until the late twentieth century. While not to put too fine an edge on it, he also held a rare Master Mariner's license to pilot any vessel, of any tonnage in any ocean.

Yet lest we stray too far afield, there is an LRH note at this juncture in his saga, and it reads in part:

"I started out writing for the pulps, writing the best I knew, writing for every mag on the stands, slanting as well as I could."

To which one might add: His earliest submissions date from the

Capt. L. Ron Hubbard in Ketchikan, Alaska, 1940, on his Alaskan Radio Experimental Expedition, the first of three voyages conducted under the Explorers Club flag.

summer of 1934, and included tales drawn from true-to-life Asian adventures, with characters roughly modeled on British/American intelligence operatives he had known in Shanghai. His early Westerns were similarly peppered with details drawn from personal experience. Although therein lay a first hard lesson from the often cruel world of the pulps. His first Westerns were soundly rejected as lacking the authenticity of a Max Brand yarn (a particularly frustrating comment given L. Ron Hubbard's Westerns came straight from his Montana homeland, while Max Brand was a mediocre New York poet named Frederick Schiller Faust, who turned out implausible six-shooter tales from the terrace of an Italian villa).

Nevertheless, and needless to say, L. Ron Hubbard persevered and soon earned a reputation as among the most publishable names in pulp fiction, with a ninety percent placement rate of first-draft manuscripts. He was also among the most prolific, averaging between seventy and a hundred thousand words a month. Hence the rumors that L. Ron Hubbard had redesigned a typewriter for faster keyboard action and pounded out manuscripts on a continuous roll of butcher paper to save the precious seconds it took to insert a single sheet of paper into manual typewriters of the day.

That all L. Ron Hubbard stories did not run beneath said byline is yet another aspect of pulp fiction lore. That is, as publishers periodically rejected manuscripts from top-drawer authors if only to avoid paying top dollar, L. Ron Hubbard and company just as frequently replied with submissions under various pseudonyms. In Ron's case, the

A MAN OF MANY NAMES

Between 1934 and 1950, L. Ron Hubbard authored more than fifteen million words of fiction in more than two hundred classic publications. To supply his fans and editors with stories across an array of genres and pulp titles, he adopted fifteen pseudonyms in addition to his already renowned L. Ron Hubbard byline.

Winchester Remington Colt
Lt. Jonathan Daly
Capt. Charles Gordon
Capt. L. Ron Hubbard
Bernard Hubbel
Michael Keith
Rene Lafayette
Legionnaire 148
Legionnaire 14830
Ken Martin
Scott Morgan
Lt. Scott Morgan
Kurt von Rachen
Barry Randolph
Capt. Humbert Reynolds

list included: Rene Lafayette, Captain Charles Gordon, Lt. Scott Morgan and the notorious Kurt von Rachen—supposedly on the lam for a murder rap, while hammering out two-fisted prose in Argentina. The point: While L. Ron Hubbard as Ken Martin spun stories of Southeast Asian intrigue, LRH as Barry Randolph authored tales of

L. Ron Hubbard, circa 1930, at the outset of a literary career that would finally span half a century.

romance on the Western range—which, stretching between a dozen genres is how he came to stand among the two hundred elite authors providing close to a million tales through the glory days of American Pulp Fiction.

In evidence of exactly that, by 1936 L. Ron Hubbard was literally leading pulp fiction's elite as president of New York's American Fiction Guild. Members included a veritable pulp hall of fame: Lester "Doc Savage" Dent, Walter "The Shadow" Gibson, and the legendary Dashiell Hammett—to cite but a few.

Also in evidence of just where L. Ron Hubbard stood within his first two years on the American pulp circuit: By the spring of 1937, he was ensconced in Hollywood, adopting a Caribbean thriller for Columbia Pictures, remembered today as *The Secret of Treasure Island*. Comprising fifteen thirty-minute episodes, the L. Ron Hubbard screenplay led to the most profitable matinée serial in Hollywood history. In accord with Hollywood culture, he was thereafter continually called upon

The 1937 Secret of Treasure Island, *a fifteen-episode serial adapted for the screen by L. Ron Hubbard from his novel,* Murder at Pirate Castle.

to rewrite/doctor scripts—most famously for long-time friend and fellow adventurer Clark Gable.

In the interim—and herein lies another distinctive chapter of the L. Ron Hubbard story—he continually worked to open Pulp Kingdom gates to up-and-coming authors. Or, for that matter, anyone who wished to write. It was a fairly unconventional stance, as markets were already thin and competition razor sharp. But the fact remains, it was an L. Ron Hubbard hallmark that he vehemently lobbied on behalf of young authors—regularly supplying instructional articles to trade journals, guest-lecturing to short story classes at George Washington University and Harvard, and even founding his own creative writing competition. It was established in 1940, dubbed the Golden Pen, and guaranteed winners both New York representation and publication in *Argosy*.

But it was John W. Campbell Jr.'s *Astounding Science Fiction* that finally proved the most memorable LRH vehicle. While every fan of L. Ron Hubbard's galactic epics undoubtedly knows the story, it nonetheless bears repeating: By late 1938, the pulp publishing magnate of Street & Smith was determined to revamp *Astounding Science Fiction* for broader readership. In particular, senior editorial director F. Orlin Tremaine called for stories with a stronger *human element*. When acting editor John W. Campbell balked, preferring his spaceship-driven tales, Tremaine enlisted Hubbard. Hubbard, in turn, replied with the genre's first truly *character-driven* works, wherein heroes are pitted not against bug-eyed monsters but the mystery and majesty of deep space itself—and thus was launched the Golden Age of Science Fiction.

The names alone are enough to quicken the pulse of any science fiction aficionado, including LRH friend and protégé, Robert Heinlein, Isaac Asimov, A. E. van Vogt and Ray Bradbury. Moreover, when coupled with LRH stories of fantasy, we further come to what's rightly been described as the foundation of every modern tale of horror: L. Ron Hubbard's immortal *Fear*. It was rightly proclaimed by Stephen King as one of the very few works to genuinely warrant that overworked term "classic"—as in: *"This is a classic tale of creeping, surreal menace and horror. . . . This is one of the really, really good ones."*

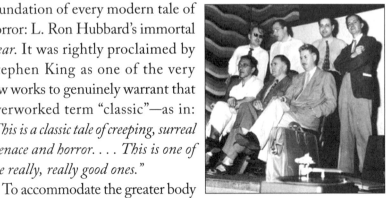

L. Ron Hubbard, 1948, among fellow science fiction luminaries at the World Science Fiction Convention in Toronto.

To accommodate the greater body of L. Ron Hubbard fantasies, Street & Smith inaugurated *Unknown*—a classic pulp if there ever was one, and wherein readers were soon thrilling to the likes of *Typewriter in the Sky* and *Slaves of Sleep* of which Frederik Pohl would declare: *"There are bits and pieces from Ron's work that became part of the language in ways that very few other writers managed."*

And, indeed, at J. W. Campbell Jr.'s insistence, Ron was regularly drawing on themes from the Arabian Nights and so introducing readers to a world of genies, jinn, Aladdin and Sinbad—all of which, of course, continue to float through cultural mythology to this day.

At least as influential in terms of post-apocalypse stories was L. Ron Hubbard's 1940 *Final Blackout*. Generally acclaimed as the finest anti-war novel of the decade and among the ten best works of the genre ever authored—here, too, was a tale that would live on in ways few other writers imagined.

Hence, the later Robert Heinlein verdict: "Final Blackout *is as perfect a piece of science fiction as has ever been written.*"

Like many another who both lived and wrote American pulp adventure, the war proved a tragic end to Ron's sojourn in the pulps. He served with distinction in four theaters and was highly decorated

Portland, Oregon, 1943; L. Ron Hubbard, captain of the US Navy subchaser PC 815.

for commanding corvettes in the North Pacific. He was also grievously wounded in combat, lost many a close friend and colleague and thus resolved to say farewell to pulp fiction and devote himself to what it had supported these many years—namely, his serious research.

But in no way was the LRH literary saga at an end, for as he wrote some thirty years later, in 1980:

"Recently there came a period when I had little to do. This was novel in a life so crammed with busy years, and I decided to amuse myself by writing a novel that was pure *science fiction."*

That work was *Battlefield Earth: A Saga of the Year 3000*. It was an immediate *New York Times* bestseller and, in fact, the first international science fiction blockbuster in decades. It was not, however, L. Ron Hubbard's magnum opus, as that distinction is generally reserved for his next and final work: The 1.2 million word *Mission Earth*.

> **Final Blackout**
> *is as perfect a piece of science fiction as has ever been written.*
>
> —Robert Heinlein

How he managed those 1.2 million words in just over twelve months is yet another piece of the L. Ron Hubbard legend. But the fact remains, he did indeed author a ten-volume *dekalogy* that lives in publishing history for the fact that each and every volume of the series was also a *New York Times* bestseller.

Moreover, as subsequent generations discovered L. Ron Hubbard through republished works and novelizations of his screenplays, the mere fact of his name on a cover signaled an international bestseller. . . . Until, to date, sales of his works exceed hundreds of millions, and he otherwise remains among the most enduring and widely read authors in literary history. Although as a final word on the tales of L. Ron Hubbard, perhaps it's enough to simply reiterate what editors told readers in the glory days of American Pulp Fiction:

He writes the way he does, brothers, because he's been there, seen it and done it!

THE STORIES FROM THE GOLDEN AGE

Your ticket to adventure starts here with the Stories from
the Golden Age collection by master storyteller L. Ron Hubbard.
These gripping tales are set in a kaleidoscope of exotic locales and brim
with fascinating characters, including some of the
most vile villains, dangerous dames and brazen heroes
you'll ever get to meet.

The entire collection of over one hundred and fifty stories is being
released in a series of eighty books and audiobooks.
For an up-to-date listing of available titles,
go to www.goldenagestories.com.

AIR ADVENTURE

Arctic Wings
The Battling Pilot
Boomerang Bomber
The Crate Killer
The Dive Bomber
Forbidden Gold
Hurtling Wings
The Lieutenant Takes the Sky

Man-Killers of the Air
On Blazing Wings
Red Death Over China
Sabotage in the Sky
Sky Birds Dare!
The Sky-Crasher
Trouble on His Wings
Wings Over Ethiopia

FAR-FLUNG ADVENTURE

SEA ADVENTURE

TALES FROM THE ORIENT

MYSTERY

FANTASY

Borrowed Glory
The Crossroads
Danger in the Dark
The Devil's Rescue
He Didn't Like Cats

If I Were You
The Last Drop
The Room
The Tramp

SCIENCE FICTION

The Automagic Horse
Battle of Wizards
Battling Bolto
The Beast
Beyond All Weapons
A Can of Vacuum
The Conroy Diary
The Dangerous Dimension
Final Enemy
The Great Secret
Greed
The Invaders

A Matter of Matter
The Obsolete Weapon
One Was Stubborn
The Planet Makers
The Professor Was a Thief
The Slaver
Space Can
Strain
Tough Old Man
240,000 Miles Straight Up
When Shadows Fall

WESTERN

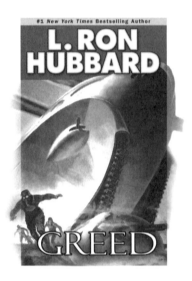